Thom Fritz

Rollabout Australia

ISBN: 1-59526-400-0

Printed in the United States of America by Llumina Press

Library of Congress Control Number: 2006904594

Dedicated to Anna

Authors Note:

My thanks go out to Bernadette Agron for her unending support and belief in me, also for her editing of an unruly manuscript.

Introduction

> Australia is a land of wonder. Like the land of Oz, it is full of mystery and magic. This island continent exhibits one of the most inhospitable environments on earth. The animals are unique, like creatures from a different planet. Australia can boast of the earliest signs of man. Furthermore, its terrain features some the oldest and most unchanged geologic features on the planet.

That sense of uniqueness sums up how I felt when I made my plans to go to Australia, and the feeling remains after I returned, and this is how I continue to feel to this day. Yet, after my return, the land down under has taken on an even deeper wonder. It truly is a land filled with mystery and magic.

Often when people get me to talking about Australia, I get a twinkle in my eyes and I have to limit the length of the conversation, because I could go on for hours. Australia is never far from my thoughts, even many years after having last seen it, and it is a subject that I never tire of. In fact, I was talking with my father not long after I returned and he suggested that I write this story down. Lo, these many years later, here it is.

This is the story of my adventure to Australia. It began as a childhood fantasy. It was not until many years later that it became a plan, and finally a reality. It was a reality that many people told me I could not accomplish.

I wanted to go to Australia, and I had no preconceived notions about what I wanted to do when I got there. So I bought a thirty-day round-trip ticket to Melbourne. I selected Melbourne because that is where a friend lived. I hoped that she could arrange to spend some time with me to help me get oriented to the city. I had no reservations. I had no tours planned. I had no specific ideas of what I wanted to see. All I wanted to do is go to Australia, that is what I did. In fact, in Australia I did a Walkabout.

I bought a t-shirt in Australia when I was visiting Phillip's Island. On the front it had a silhouette of a kangaroo against a blue and purple background, with the words "Walkabout Australia" in bold lettering. It came to be a symbol of my adventure. I treasured the shirt and wore it daily, until it was threadbare and no longer wearable. A Walkabout is a journey of self-discovery—like a Native American vision quest. The sheer amount of territory I traversed gives testimony to the challenging nature of my journey. My travels took me to Melbourne, Sydney, Adelaide, Alice Springs and finally Uluru.

What people will find interesting about my Walkabout is that it took place in a wheelchair. Thus, I have dubbed it a Rollabout rather than a Walkabout.

Often people are amazed, and a little bit skeptical about my story not only because I undertook the adventure with a disability and in a wheelchair, but also because I departed with just a ticket to Australia and no other plans. I, too, am sometimes truly amazed.

In this day of the Internet, a technology that was not available then, I've collected a treasure of facts about Australia. I have included in the back of this book a list of web addresses about the many things I encountered while I was there. This list is by no means to be taken as representing "Australia" in its completeness, there are thousands and thousands of web pages about Australia.

Thom Fritz

Contents:

1

Pursuing a Dream

Ever since I was a boy, I wanted to go to Australia. At about the age of eight or so, I began reading books about the island continent, Australia. At the age of twelve, when my mind had become mature enough to begin to have positive dreams, I dreamed about Australia. Many days I spent thinking about Australia. I even got in trouble at school for not paying attention in class, because I was daydreaming about my whimsical adventures I would have there.

Australia is a place of wonder, and when I was a boy it beckoned as a land like Oz, full of mystery and magic. I read that it had one of the most inhospitable environments on Earth, and even though I didn't really understand what that meant--"inhospitable environments"--it sounded like something special. The animals I read about were so different that I even thought they might really be from another planet. I had read that the earliest signs of man were discovered in Australia, and again, I didn't really understand what that meant. I read that Australia exhibits the oldest and least changed geologic features of the planet. The more I read the more intrigued I became.

There was one book in particular I read over and over as a boy, though I can no longer recall the name. I have since tried many times to find the book, without success. I just remember the little creature that the main character, a young girl, carried around in the top pocket of her shirt. It had big reddish brown eyes that were about the size of dimes. I don't remember what the furry little thing was or what she called it, and it doesn't matter now. I don't know exactly what I envisioned, but it was some kind of marsupial. The image I had in my mind was so cute and lovable. The idea of finding a creature like that and keeping it for a pet tickled me, and I pledged to myself that I would go to Australia one day to find it.

This was a promise to myself that would never come to pass. I have spent much of my life making plans that would never be fulfilled. This was the first of many promises, dreams and plans that I remember never came to be. One could say I suffered from an unconscious desire to control my confusing environment, though a complete inability to do so. Yet, I continued on living my life and achieving what I could. I hadn't learned the notion that if one holds onto a belief strongly enough that it can manifest into reality. I had been taught that life just happens and to take it as it comes, yet, obviously, I knew there was more to belief.

While growing up, the constant drone of radio talk shows was in the background. I heard the words, yet much of the time it was just sound. My mother turned on the radio more for background noise than as a listening program. I rarely agreed with the talk show host's viewpoints and often found it difficult to reconcile the views I heard with how I pictured the world to be. I felt very out of touch with the outside world back then, but deep down I knew that the world had to be better than the closed-minded version of the talk show host. Since my mother would turn on this radio station as soon as she got up, and, except for mealtime, kept it on until she went to bed, the noise was always there.

There was one radio commentator however that I did enjoy. His name was Paul Harvey. His was a news program that came on every day at noon. He delivered the news with a sardonic flair that was so humorous it seemed almost a joke, yet he was quite believable. His one-liner style of delivery captured my attention. One day he gave a brief news report that the Australian government was distributing forty-acre parcels of land, free and clear, to anyone who would homestead without outside help for five years. I heard the brief news report only once, so I didn't know if I was hearing it correctly. I called the radio station to find out if I had heard him right. The people at the radio station said that indeed was what he had said, but they did not know if he was accurate.

That news item had struck a chord in me because in brief snippets of conversation between the adults in the family, I had heard them talking about my grandparents, who had migrated into Saskatchewan, Canada, from North Dakota, to homestead a section and a half, roughly a thousand acres, or one-and-a-half square miles, of land. When I was sixteen a cousin and I visited Canada and stayed with a distant relative for six weeks. During that time I got to see the original, abandoned structure—the remnants of the house that my grandparents had built. A small two-story wood house made of rough-hewn timber--weather beaten and warped, from years of rain, stripped of what little paint there had been, and sun bleached. The rooms were tiny and claustrophobic and it was hard to imagine that my grandparents had lived and farmed in this humble abode, withstood harsh forty-degree-below winters and one-hundred-and-twenty-degree summers, raised a family (one of which had been my mother), and made a life for themselves. The house stood alone at the end of an overgrown, deeply rutted entry road that led off from a seldom-used road about twelve miles out of Corona, Canada. For miles around there was absolutely nothing. In fact, one could turn three-hundred-and-sixty degrees in a circle and see nothing but prairie and open land, with not even a hill. My grandparents had truly been pioneers. I did not know the harsh reality of how it was, and did not know if I had what it took to be a pioneer, but I wanted to test myself. I knew nothing about homesteading, except for what I had overheard, but I thought, if my grandparents could do it, then so could I.

The visions of what my life would be like danced through my head--happy, content, unbreaking visions. I could picture the farm that would rise up from dust, the house I would build, and the many friends and neighbors I would have. The dream was alive and captivating in its splendor, it danced and it danced.

My plan was that when I turned eighteen I would seek out the details of the brief report I had heard years before on the radio and would be the proud and worthy owner of land in Australia. I was at the age when girls were transforming themselves into women and the dreams took on a whole new frame of reference: I could picture myself sitting with my wife in a porch swing on the front porch of my house, overlooking my land, and my children, numbering five or six, would be playing in the yard. I could even picture what my wife looked like. She had a head of tight, wavy auburn hair so plentiful it could be worn as an Afro, and she parted it loosely down the middle and tied it with two colorful ribbons, which she changed the color of daily. Her face was full and annular, covered with freckles, with green eyes, and a smile that spoke of contentment and happiness. Life was static and complete.

But, in the manner of the lives of many young people, my life kept happening and other things attracted and absorbed and swallowed my attention, dreams and plans. The Australian homesteading dream was all but forgotten. All the pressing needs, wants and have-to's of my adolescence started to become nightmares of confusion and self-doubt. Life got so complicated around that time that I started to become very self-conscious and uncomfortable when people were watching me. I spent most of the time by myself. Yet, in spite of my inner turmoil, I was determined to go on and make something of my life.

Many years later, with many experiences having come and gone, I was working at an Independent Living Center (WCIL) as an MFCC Intern therapist, counseling people with disabilities. However, suddenly the funding for the position was withdrawn and I was out of work. This came as somewhat of a blessing in disguise, for I could now make plans for my future.

I was twenty-nine years old and, as the age of thirty approached, I was thinking about what I had done in my life and where I was going. I had some money saved up and traveling was something I wanted to do from time to time. I figured that because of the nature of my disability, I probably would not have the strength and ability to travel by myself for many more years. Various destinations came to mind: Europe, Africa, South America, and even many places here in the United States. But deep down inside a little voice kept calling to me: "Australia . . . . Go to Australia. It's where you've wanted to go ever since you were a boy, don't you remember? That magical land, known as Australia."

So once again, the itch to go to Australia preoccupied my mind. That little voice triggered the old memory of the long lost dream. Maybe I had never actually buried the dream as deeply as I thought I had. The layoff became an unexpected opportunity to realize it. An adventure awaited me and I was finally ready to take it on.

> Part of the reason the dream became buried was that when I was sixteen years old I was finally diagnosed with the disease that had been plaguing me throughout my childhood, adolescence and adulthood. I am afflicted with this condition today. It is called Friedreich's Ataxia.

Friedreich's Ataxia is a slowly progressive disorder of the nervous system, muscles and the predominant aspect being the deterioration of the Cerebellum. The disorder, named for the physician who first identified it in the early 1860's, results in the inability to coordinate voluntary muscle movements--the basic definition of ataxia; lack of coordination. If a healthy individual drinks too much alcohol and begins stumbling, is very uncoordinated and slurs their words, this person has one of the main symptoms of ataxia, albeit temporary. The person with ataxia, in contrast, is not necessarily drunk nor has he or she consumed any alcohol. This condition is caused by degeneration of nerve tissue in the cerebellum, spinal cord and of nerves that extend to peripheral areas such as the arms and legs, not from alcohol. (When I was first diagnosed I remember saying to the doctor to just "draw the extra alcohol out of my brain and I will be fine.") It affects both upper and lower limbs, and the head and neck. There is also a particular loss of the sensations of touch and pressure in the arms and legs. Unlike some neurological diseases, Friedreich's Ataxia does not affect mental capacity.

For me, it started, or became noticeable, when I was six years old. A doctor noticed, while examining me one day, that my gait was somewhat unusual. Thus began a long and sometimes unpleasant series of examinations. The first one was not too difficult. He merely had me walk up and down the corridor several times to watch me. I had the first signs of what later would be called "the ataxia gait," a signature widening of the gait to be able to keep my balance. Throughout the years, it continued to gradually, but markedly, get worse, or change, as I would rather say.

A fuller diagnosis came from a weeklong stay in the hospital for a series of tests and procedures. One of these was called a Pneumoencephalogram. It is a barbarous test administered before the high-tech and painless MRI was discovered. Air was injected into my spinal column and I was strapped firmly into a chair, then turned upside down and every which way to take x-rays of my brain. During the procedure the technicians would not help me and I wound up vomiting all over myself, because the air displacing the spinal fluid, as I would be turned from one position to another, moved shifting the air pocket to another portion of my brain and this would cause severe nausea. To top this off, I had to lie flat on my back for twenty-four hours. This was so uncomfortable for me at the time because I was used to sleeping on my side. In the end it offered one more layer of confirmation to the diagnosis the first doctor had given.

For much of my childhood I was "treated" by numerous doctors for "symptoms": the irregular gait, the deteriorating coordination, the failing balance. They said they "knew" what they were doing. Yet, they seemed endlessly involved in finding out what they thought, in their "medical opinion," was the cause for my physical changes. Subsequently they subjected me to a myriad of tests and procedures; some almost torturous, others routine and monotonous. I could have told them something was wrong if they had bothered to ask.

At one point I was sent to yet another doctor, for a referential symptom-related problem, an irregular heart beat. After finishing with his tests, he sent me to still another doctor. This doctor was a Neurological Diagnostician. He merely ran a finger up my spine, took a look at my feet, which were misshapen because I had very high arches, and walked over to a shelf in his office, opened a book, and without leafing through the pages, pointed to a description of the condition I had. It was all so simple and basic. The amount of knowledge and experience he had was by far and away worthy of respect. I will always be grateful to this man, although I don't even remember his name. By giving my disability a name, he ended the torture and experiments of my childhood.

At the same time, the sheer magnitude of this knowledge, which in a sense was like handing me a death sentence, was devastating to hear and take in. No young man of sixteen should ever have to hear that he has an incurable disease that will someday kill him.

The changes affected every area of my life growing up, from running and playing and being physically active and playing sports, to having lessened coordination when it came to working with my hands and playing musical instruments, to relationships with people and being social (I was often ridiculed and made fun of by my peers for being different), to my self-confidence and self-esteem. It did not stop with my body, and took a big toll on my self-respect and sense of being in and part of the world. I became very self-conscious and my lack of confidence in myself became increasingly evident. There was no area of my life that was not affected by the disease.

Yet, in spite of the changes, or maybe because of the changes that were happening to my body and emotions, I didn't lose any of the inner drive to live and experience my life to the fullest. Maybe, it was a naïve childhood innocence, or maybe it was the many times I had hit my head, crashed my bike, missed a handhold on the monkey bars, took a misstep because of my coordination, tripped and fell down a flight of stairs, or just lost my balance. All this, I feel, made me almost oblivious to the changes going on. That naïve childhood innocence or what ever it was, though, became a determination to be who I was, and am, and to live as "normal" a life as I could.

When the situation presented itself and I became determined to go to Australia, my physical changes were at a level that I needed to use a wheelchair. Actually, I had been using a wheelchair for almost ten years. My coordination was at the level where I could write, but only I could read it, and my speech was such that I sometimes had to repeat myself. I knew that I would not have the strength and fortitude to take such an adventure on my own for many more years, or perhaps not at all, and grasped this opportunity when it presented itself.

2

Preparations

It was a bold notion that I could possibly travel to Australia, in my physical condition. Based on my decision I knew I needed to do some planning, though I knew I didn't want to plan too much. I had never been one to spend a lot of time planning. I preferred to take events as they came. It was clear to me, however, that I did need to organize a few necessary steps to bring this dream to fruition.

For starters, I needed a passport and a visa. For the passport, I needed my birth certificate, or a copy. All the digging through my papers and files did not make it appear, even though I thought if I dug enough, it would. I spent the better part of a day in City Hall, downtown Los Angeles, which is always crowded, waiting in line to get a copy of my original birth certificate. Despite all my efforts, they did not even give it to me that day. It was mailed to me in a timely fashion, two or three weeks later. Once I had my birth certificate I then moved on to the federal building and waited in another line to get my passport. As I expected, it also took two or three weeks to receive. Once I had my passport, I then could go to the Australian consulate and apply for a visa. To my surprise, they stamped it then and there.

Looking into the prices of air fare to Australia, I found that the tickets were fairly high and relativity the same for all of the airlines. Twelve-hundred dollars was a steep price to pay, but it was because of the time of year I wanted to fly. Luckily, I found a ticket agency that sold tickets to students at discount prices--for four-hundred dollars less. I was not actually a student, but I had recently finished my graduate studies in psychology, and the agency bent the rules enough to fit me in. My ticket was part of a block of tickets that had been sold to a tour group, but was unused. So, instead of flying with an empty seat, the ticket agency sold me that empty seat, saving me money and making a profit for both the agency and the airline.

I had no plans, other than flying to Australia. No tours planned. No rail tickets. No cities that I especially wanted to see. All I wanted to do was to go to Australia. And that is what I was finally going to do. I had, a round-trip ticket to Melbourne.

I had a friend I had kept corresponding with over several years, who lived in Australia. We had met at an

Elizabeth Kubler-Ross seminar on Death and Dying in Tucson, Arizona, when she was thumbing rides around America.

On the last day of the seminar, a farewell lunch was held for all attendees. I couldn't help but notice a devastatingly attractive young woman, whom I had admired earlier in the week, get up to leave. Her name was Anna. I wanted to catch her before she disappeared for good. So I quickly put down what I was eating, caught up with her and invited her to come stay with me in Venice, while she visited Los Angeles. She said she had already been to Los Angeles, and that she had been frightened the entire time she was there. She showed me a whistle she had carried on a chain around her neck and said that nearly the entire time she had been in Los Angeles she had held the whistle between her lips--ready to blow. I chuckled, because I knew that for a timid, self-conscious, good-looking young woman such as her, Los Angeles could be an intimidating city. She assured me though that she had my address from the seminar list and that she would write to me once she settled down. At the time, she planned to settle down someplace in the US or Canada. She ended up living in Ontario, Canada for several years before finally moving back to Australia.

I wrote to Anna to ask if she would he able to pick me up at the airport. She lived in Melbourne, and because I had no idea what Australia was like, and not knowing what her schedule would be like, I thought the sight of the one person I knew there would help ease my introduction to the county. Still, I wasn't worried, if she couldn't meet me. I figured on holing up in an inexpensive hotel or a maybe a youth hostel for a couple of days to get grounded and to get my bearings. Then I'd figure out what I was going to do.

In the weeks before the trip I had done some research and looked into the youth hostels of the YHA organization--an association of youth hostels located in different countries around the world. A youth hostel offers dormitory style sleeping arrangements and a communal kitchen and laundry facilities. Because it is nothing really fancy, it is much less expensive, between ten and eighteen dollars.

I always thought that paying a lot of money for a room is both crazy and overindulgent. I just wanted a bed, a place to sleep and to stay out of the weather in a relativity safe room without the risk of being hassled for being indigent. Sleep is a simple, basic need. When you are asleep, the furnishings don't matter. The way I see it, I will be asleep.

The proposition of holing up in a motel or hotel or youth hostel was a curious idea that I found kind of appealing. At the same time, I found the idea somewhat unnerving. Here I would be in a new city, and not just a new city, but actually in a new city in an entirely different country, halfway around the world. Would I be able to handle this? What if Australia was very inaccessible, as I had heard from people who had traveled there? I just didn't want to believe this, and because it was really something I didn't want to think about, I was able to put it out of my mind. But still . . . I asked myself if I would I be able to deal with this in my distant adventure in spite of all the good things that would happen? Would facing the unknown make me turn around and run home with my tail between my legs? These questions kept running through my head. My anxiety rose steadily as the days grew closer. Was I really going to be able to do this?

I had not heard from Anna long after I sent my first letter to her . I wrote her again. I didn't know what to expect as I waited each day for the mail. Each day hurrying out to the mailbox when the mail came to see if I got a letter, I had to walk back into the house with disappointment written all over my face. Three days before my departure date, I received a telegram with nine important and very welcome words, "I'LL PICK YOU UP AT THE AIRPORT, LOVE ANNA."

I was ecstatic. This short communication was like getting a ten-page letter with a written guarantee that I was going to have a good time. Although I didn't know Anna that well, I felt very relieved. At least one unknown had been resolved. I now knew that my introduction to Australia was not going to be totally anxiety ridden. On the first day, I was scheduled to land in Australia in the morning, and now I was hoping to spend the day with Anna, gathering some inside knowledge about my destination.

I later discovered that at the time I sent my letters to Anna, the Australian postal workers were on strike throughout the entire country and the only way my friend could think of to contact me was to send a telegram. She said later that the letters had come to the post office, where a volunteer had spent time sorting through some of the mail.

As the day of my departure grew near, my final days at the agency where I worked part-time as a Peer Counselor were filled with both excitement about the adventure that awaited me and an impending sadness about leaving the center. The prospect of turning over my clients to another therapist was not helping. My clients' lives had become part of mine, and hopefully I, or my perceptions and helpful ideas, had become part of theirs as well.

When I wasn't working at the center, I was preparing for the trip. I was looking at a month of rugged travel ahead of me, and I didn't have a clue what to expect. I assumed there would be coin-operated Laundromats when I got there, so I only took a few days' changes of clothes, and some personal items. The process of choosing what clothes to take and what to leave behind was not that difficult. I've never had a need to make a fashion statement.

My next consideration was how to transport my baggage. I needed to carry my clothes and other items with me on my trip, but if I carried them in an ordinary suitcase, I would not be able to move around freely in my wheelchair. I would not be able to push the wheelchair and carry my luggage at the same time. I considered a few creative approaches, but the one I settled on was a modification of a backpack. A backpack is usually attached to an aluminum frame and the straps that wrap around one's body attach to it. Instead of using the aluminum frame, I used some seatbelt-like straps, and fashioned them into loops. Next, I attached them to the backpack, and from there, onto the push handles of my wheelchair. It looked a little unusual, but, at the time, I didn't care. I was going to Australia. No worrying about what other people thought. What did matter was that the backpack served its functional purpose.

I rigged another bag with metal hooks that would hang below the seat of my wheelchair, between my legs. This would carry my wheelchair tools and a few odd pieces of equipment that I might need. It would also serve as a counter-balance so that the backpack, which would be heavy with clothes, would not tilt me over backwards. I also made provisions for another bag that I carried on my lap, which would also help to keep me from tipping over backwards.

One of the pockets of the backpack was reserved especially for this little, ugly, stuffed dog, which traveled with me the entire trip. I pulled it out each and every time I made my bed for the night. This little pet had been given to me as a sign of friendship by one of the counselors at the same seminar where I had met Anna several years before. My stuffed companion was a caricature of one of those dogs with too much skin. One of its ears had been chewed off by one of my dogs and I had sewn it back on and wrapped it with a symbolic bandage. This little dog was so ugly it was cute. It had been given to me while I was going through some intense work during the seminar. It became even more significant to me for another reason, because of the dog that had torn off the little stuffed dogs ear in the first place. The real-life dog was a ninety-pound pitbull that I had named, "Shotgun." The reason I named him that was because he had a spot of Brindle, mottled brown and black markings, around his tail that made him look like he had been shot in the rear with buckshot. Like the stuffed dog, he was so ugly he was cute. After he died, there were times I felt a little uneasy, you might say somewhat insecure not having a dog around, and I took to a backwards development that I didn't share with a lot of people, of sleeping with this little, ugly, stuffed dog.

My wheelchair was old, old in wheelchair years, four or five years old, and I had made some modifications in order to render it better and more comfortable. It needed to be carefully gone over to make certain that all the screws, nuts and bolts were tight. I even put an extra special lining inside the tires to ensure against flats. Even having done this simple preparation, I was to have unforeseen problems later.

I had everything together I thought, my ticket, my passport and visa, my luggage, and my souped-up wheelchair. Now I just had to wait for the day I was to leave. As the days passed and my departure date grew closer and closer I got more nervous and anxious, but even more excited. This was going to be not just an ordinary trip, but an extraordinary adventure! This idea kept coming back to me over and over, and I know now, looking back on it, that this is why it was such an adventure. Because I so strongly willed it to be.

3

The Flight Down Under

The date came for my departure and I found myself sitting at the curb in front of the international terminal at LAX. I wanted no lingering goodbyes, so I insisted on just being dropped off at the airport. I had time as I sat there to go over the mental checklist in my head.

Let's see . . . I have my passport, right? I remember it was such a hassle to go to the federal building and stand in line, but I didn't really trust the mail to get it to me in time. Then there was another line before that to get my birth certificate downtown. Let me check my pocket to make sure I have it, and I want to see it. I felt in the pocket where I had placed it and pulled it out to make sure, yes . . . here it is, I have it right here. I should check on my visa and spending money, I'll have to pull each out to check and make sure. Yes, they are right here where I put them. I better check on my ticket, Oh no! . . . it's not here in the pocket where I thought I had placed it. Panicking slightly, I began looking through my other pockets and finally through my bag. With a sigh of relief I found it tucked in my bag and remembered that I had put it there to make sure I didn't lose it. I laughed at myself, because I had almost lost it trying not to lose it.

The international terminal was an enormous structure, furnished with brown carpets, shiny black counters and high ceilings. The line leading up to the ticket counter was long, very long, and it moved forward at a snail's pace. I began to wonder if I would make it to the plane on time. As I crept slowly forward I pushed the backpack and my tool and equipment bag, which were now on the floor in front of me, with the front of my wheelchair. The bags would presumably need to be loaded as luggage. Once in awhile someone else in line would help me slide them forward. The other bag I carried on my lap, along with my Levi jacket. It was the only jacket I took on the trip, which I learned later, was not the best idea. Australia is very close to Antarctica and I had no idea it could get so cold.

After what seemed like an eternity, I finally reached the ticket counter.

"Who is traveling with you?" the woman behind the counter asked, as many people often do after looking at me and noticing that I am in a wheelchair. It's a common assumption for people who are unfamiliar with disabilities to think that we all need complete care by someone else because we're obviously unable to take care of ourselves.

"No one. I am traveling alone," I growled, while trying to smile. I didn't want my annoyance over her question to show, though I imagine I broadcasted it loud and clear. The woman behind the ticket counter--who looked to be well into her sixties, with a face wrinkled by time, parched and ready to blow away--scrutinized me and the ticket carefully again and began shaking her head.

The seat I had selected at the travel agency was up against the bulkhead, or in the first row of seats. I deliberately had chosen this location because it affords the luxury of plenty of foot room.

The ticket agent pointed to the screen--which I obviously could not see, because we were on opposite sides of the counter--and blurted out in a high-pitched, sing-song kind of voice, "You can't sit there." She reminded me of a little kid going "naner, naner, naner." "That's right in the row of seats before an emergency exit," she continued, "I am just going to have to assign you to a different seat." Then, as if she had been saving her best ammunition for last, she took aim in her best sarcastic voice and said, "Unless you can get up and aid other passengers in the event of an emergency, if there is one"

I scowled, gave her one of those "very funny" looks and irritably shook my head. She gave me a different seat.

With the new seat assignment I proceeded to the gate, deep inside the international terminal. As I headed down a long walkway I looked at a clock on the wall and noticed, to my surprise, I had a good half hour before boarding. Even though it had taken what seemed like forever to get to the ticket counter, I still had plenty of time.

I was a little nervous and anxious while I waited to board the plane. I am always a bit uneasy in unknown situations, although people often don't see this, because I figure, "Life is going to happen. Take it as it comes," so I don't let myself get too rattled.

Being excited and a little fidgety, I struck up a conversation with a woman next to me. We were both waiting to board the plane. As we began talking, she asked what was taking me to Australia and who I was going to see and stay with. And then she asked if I was traveling by myself.

Excitedly I began talking about my fascination with Australia, starting back at eight years of age or so, and all the books I had read about Australia and how I used to get in trouble in class for daydreaming about Australia and how I had planned to migrate to Australia and how the dreams of Australia became buried because of being confronted with my disability and dealing with the unpredictable nature of my disease and how I had gone back to school at age 26, against proclamations that I was too old to go back to school, and received by Bachelors and Masters degrees in psychology and was interning to become a MFCC and how I had been employed as a Peer Counselor at an independent living center working with other people like myself with disabilities and how I had been let go because of lack of funding and decided to use this opportunity to fulfill the buried dream of going to Australia, which had risen over a few years. I went on to tell her that I was traveling alone and that I had a ticket only to Australia and didn't have any other plans than to be picked up at the airport in Melbourne by a friend I had met in Arizona at a workshop and was hoping to spend some time with her. This all came out in a rapid succession in an excited gush of words.

We continued to talk and I learned her name was Rosemary. She was returning to her family in Australia from Canada, where her birth family was from. She had met her husband, an Australian who had been traveling on business, in her early twenties in Canada, and now had three boys aged thirteen, fifteen and seventeen. She told me they lived in a suburb just outside of Melbourne, called Brighton. She wrote down her name and address and invited me to visit and possibly stay with them for a few days. I later found out this area was considered the Beverly Hills of Melbourne.

Our conversation was cut short with an announcement that boarding would begin. As is usually the case, I was the first to board.

There was a whole group of baggage handlers and flight attendants, many more than there needed to be, who gathered around me, hovering like mother hens, at the mouth of the plane. They helped me from my wheelchair and onto a skinny aisle chair, a narrow utility dolly-type apparatus with a thinly padded seat, and carried me, like they were struggling with a 300 pound refrigerator, onto the plane. Then they helped me transfer from the aisle chair to the seat on the airplane.

Once I was settled in, and the other passengers had boarded, we took off. The first few minutes were routine, and after the emergency instructions, they always give on planes, one of the flight attendants stepped up to me and asked how they could be of assistance helping me to the restroom. Did they need to carry me to the restroom? I explained that they didn't because I had a leg bag, and padded my leg. But I did say they might need to help with the food.

I dug my ticket out of my bag and was looking at it, still hardly believing that I was really on an airplane heading for Australia. It brought to mind a conversation that I had had with a friend about a week before I was to leave. We were both five or six beers into the evening when we began talking about the length of the flight. It would be a twenty-hour flight. I was scheduled to leave LAX on a Wednesday afternoon and scheduled to land in Melbourne on Friday morning, with a fifteen-hour flight to New Zealand, where the plane would lay-over for four hours, and then fly the remaining hour to Melbourne.

"What!" He exclaimed, looking at me perplexed, "What happened to Thursday?"

I explained to him that the plane would be crossing the Date Line. Again, he gave me that puzzled look, as if to say, “What is that?”

"An invisible line jogging around the world dividing one day from the next. A concept I never fully understood," I said. By now, I could tell that the alcohol was beginning, well, not just beginning, to fuzz both our brains.

“Well, ask the flight attendant where the missing day went," he turned to me, with a glazed look in his eyes and laughed. It was as if he had asked some kind of profound question.

With this conversation in mind, I decided to ask. I knew it was an inane question, but I had agreed. So, with tongue-in-cheek, I asked.

"Excuse me," I said, getting the flight attendant’s attention, "I was looking at my ticket and there seems to be a date discrepancy. It says here we fly out the afternoon of the 15th and land the morning of the 17th. I don't get it. Where did that missing day go?"

"We cross the Date Line," she said matter-of-factly smiling, as if trying not to laugh. She probably got questions like this all the time.

Knowing I was going to lose a day added to my feeling that I was leaving one world and entering another. It almost felt like the plane was taking me out time altogether. My orientation in time is not always in the here and now and this added perception further loosened the bolts keeping me grounded in time. I was reminded of an old TV program where a plane had flown into a storm and flew back in time. Flying thousands of miles in just a few short hours in a sense felt like time travel. Although I rationally knew this wasn't really time travel, it managed to disorientate me.

The in-flight movie was unmemorable and the lights in the aisles of the cabin were eventually dimmed. My mind kept trying to imagine what I could expect when I landed. The words, I AM GOING TO AUSTRALIA, screamed over and over in my head. Finally sleep overcame me, rather fitfully. As I faded in and out of consciousness, there were a few overhead reading lights on, sprinkled throughout the cabin, and the flight attendants seemed to be floating up and down the aisle, responding periodically to passenger call lights in the semi-darkness. I envisioned ghosts wandering up and down the aisles, haunting passengers at random, adding to an unreal feeling that the plane was entering another dimension.

I guess I had fallen into a deeper sleep than I thought because suddenly I was awakened by one of the flight attendants. She was gently shaking me by the shoulder and asking me to put my seat back into the upright position and to make sure my seat belt was fastened. I groggily asked what was going on and she announced that the plane was landing in Tahiti for an hour. I had not known about this stop. She said that the plane needed to be refueled and restocked and that I would be carried off the plane where I would then use an airport wheelchair.

The plane did not pull up to a gate and two men in airport-type looking overalls carried me, like a sack of potatoes or an old carpet bound for the trash receptacle. They carried me--one porter in front, holding me under my legs, and another behind, carrying me under my shoulders--down to the tarmac, put me sloppily into a wheelchair and pushed it into the airport.

I asked where the bathroom was and was promptly told that the handicapped bathroom was separate from the regular men's restroom, as if this mattered. Most likely, out of a need to be politically correct, they had to make the difference apparent. The handicapped restroom was a closet. It had a portable toilet and plumbing pipe mounted on one wall for a grab bar. The door was a piece of hinged plywood with a push bar lock for holding the door closed on the outside, but no lock on the inside.

The brief stay in the airport was basically uneventful. I took the time to have a cigarette or two. I noticed that hardly any of the other passengers were smoking, even though smoking was allowed in the airport. I remember thinking it kind of odd. I couldn't be so alone in my addiction. Or could I?

The terminal had high ceilings, maybe eighteen feet, which made it seem larger than it actually was. The terminal was about two-hundred feet square, separated into two rooms. One room had vending machines along one wall and had a few rickety tables to sit at while "enjoying" the fine food from the vending machines. On the other side were rows of playground benches where waiting passengers could sit In about forty-five minutes, we were ushered back onto the plane to resume our flight.

It wasn't long before we landed for our scheduled layover in New Zealand. It was either Auckland or Christ Church. The layover was between about 6 a.m. and 10 a.m. There was really no point in trying to see anything in New Zealand, I figured that by the time I went through customs or whatever lines I needed to go through, got a taxi, went into town, and got back, I'd miss the plane. So, I sat in the airport and drank coffee.

I struck up a conversation with two men. Both were returning to Australia from the US. They introduced themselves as Paul and Dave. Paul was from Australia originally and Dave had moved to Australia in the early 70's, on one the very land grants I had dreamed of owning when I was fourteen years old . They told me that the reason the plane laid over in New Zealand was because the Australian government forbade the airlines from flying over Aboriginal lands before 9:00; it was a good will gesture, they said, in giving the land back to the Aborigines. I did not know whether to believe them or not. Later I found out that they were indeed pulling my leg. Dave gave me his phone number and said to give him a call after I got settled.

4

Melbourne - Home Away From Home

It was a routine landing at the Melbourne airport. The plane seemed to have been traveling for a long time on the taxiway. I asked the flight attendant about this and she said that the runways were out about one-and-a- half kilometers, or maybe two, from the terminal.

As the plane rolled to a stop at the gate and the gangway was put into place at the side of the aircraft, my heart felt ready to pop out of my chest. What kept racing through my mind was the fact that I was actually in Australia, in the southern hemisphere of the earth, halfway around the world. I was anxious, but very excited to find myself firmly planted in the land that was once only a dream.

I had no idea what to expect, but I did know that life looked a lot different here . The very ground felt alive. The air tingled and buzzed and had a different, fresh, tantalizing scent to it. The lights seemed brighter. The people moved more freely. People were friendlier. And, I thought I could hear bubbling laughter in the background. And I wasn't even off the plane yet.

Once off the airplane, I went with the other passengers to get my bags. The luggage came down the conveyor belt and instead of moving onto a turnstile, the luggage just piled up at the base of the conveyor belt. An attendant sorted out the luggage and helped me arrange my bags on the back of my wheelchair and between my legs. After all the passengers had collected their baggage we were ushered towards customs, where our possessions were x-rayed and we were screened with a metal detector. The entire process seemed strange because we had all been screened in Los Angeles before we left. As my turn came, I set the bag on my lap on the conveyor and unloaded the heavy backpack from the back of my wheelchair and ran them through the x-ray machine, but I had forgotten about the bag under the wheelchair. The screener mentioned it and I disconnected it and sent it through the x-ray machine, where it set off detectors. The screener pointed out a shape on the screen that corresponded with an item in the bag. He thought it looked suspicious, but I knew what it was even before I opened the bag. Digging through the contents I pulled out a well-worn pair of channel locks, used for the larger nuts on my wheelchair. When I showed the screener the pliers, he just laughed. This encounter took a few minutes and instead of pulling me aside, the screener just held up the line. The other passengers were grumbling as the line moved forward again.

From the customs area all the new arriving passengers lined up to pay an arrival fee. I had never heard of an arrival fee to enter a country before, although I suppose it is a common practice—another revenue-gathering tax. From here, we headed out the doors to the release area, where people waited to greet the arriving passengers.

"Thom! Thom! Thom!" I heard, or at least, I thought I heard, my name being called.

All the passengers were crowded around me and it was difficult to see above people's chests from a sitting position. People make better doors than they do windows.

"Thom, Thom, over here!" I heard again, and finally, peering between and around the people, I saw my friend, Anna, waving her hands frantically over her head, trying to get my attention.

Anna wore a bright blue down jacket, purple blouse with narrow gray stripes, jeans and western boots, covered with sheepskin. Her hair, tight, wavy, and what I call frizzy, was longer and pulled to the sides, in a very becoming sort of way. She had a big smile on her face. I could see the freckles even from a distance. She had said in one of her letters that she had gained a lot of weight, but if she had, she had either lost it or had a different idea of what "gained a lot of weight" meant. To me she looked the same as in the picture she had sent. In fact, I had no trouble picking her out. The picture had not done her real justice, though. She was much prettier in person.

I made my way through the crowd, trying not to run into anyone with my wheelchair, I met her about half way and she bounded into my arms. We hugged as though we were old friends separated by years of hardship, and in a way we were old friends, from our letters. Though we had met only once, for a brief conversation, it felt comfortable being with her again. We threw the usual compliments back and forth that one gives at meeting after a long separation and fell into that comfortable rhythm of old friends.

We stepped out onto the curb in front of the arrival terminal. It overlooked several parking structures. She had parked in an outside lot and she offered to get the car and bring it around to the front of the airport, where we were. Because I had just gotten off a twenty-hour flight, the last thing I wanted at that point was to crawl back into a confined space like a car. I told her I would rather move around for awhile.

I made sure my bags were in place and we proceeded through the parking lot to her car, which was halfway to the back of the lot. The air was fresh and clean and a bit cool so I put on my jacket and she laughed, asking if I had brought a thicker coat.

When I told her that this was the only coat I brought, she just shrugged and shook her head. The air was cool and clean and I could feel the moisture in it. It looked like it was going to rain any moment so we hurried toward the car.

The layout of the parking lot was different than what I was unaccustomed to. The arrows on the pavement were in the wrong lanes and the right-turn-only lanes were pointing left instead of right, and vice versa. This entered my subconscious without really registering in my mind.. When we arrived at the car, I rolled up to the right side of the car, thinking I was rolling up to the passenger door. She chuckled and chided me and asked me if I was going to drive. I looked at her, uncomprehending, and then I looked through the window and saw the steering wheel where I had not expected it to be. Suddenly the markings in the parking lot came to mind and I understood why they had not registered as being right. I remembered then that in Australia people drove on the left, the other side; the wrong side. To my thinking, having grown up in the United States, driving on the right was the right side of the road, and driving on left side, as in Australia, was the wrong side of the road. Realizing my mistake, I then rolled around to the other side and climbed in.

She started the car and reached over to put it in gear, when I noticed another difference. Instead of having the gear shift to my left, when sitting in the passenger seat, it was to my right and she was reaching to her left for the gear shift. She backed out and began driving through the parking lot on the left side of the road. Cars passed us, coming from the opposite direction, on the right, and although I got used to this fairly quickly, I had an odd sensation something was wrong. It was not until we pulled out onto the main road exiting the airport and rounded the corner that I got the biggest shock. It felt like we were turning down the wrong side of the street and we would run head-on into oncoming traffic.

I'd repeatedly get a bearing on traveling in the left lane until we'd round another corner and I would again get the sensation that we were turning down the wrong side of the street and we would run head-on into oncoming traffic. It was terribly disconcerting and it seemed I would never get comfortable with traveling on the other side of the road.

The airport was beyond even the outskirts of Melbourne. Anna took a circuitous route around the city instead of driving through it, explaining that this route would save time. The area of the city we traveled through looked like any other large sprawling city in America. The airport was surrounded by industrial- looking buildings that appeared commercial and plain. But they were well built and looked as if they could withstand a hurricane.

We pulled onto a busy throughway and I immediately noticed a difference in the construction of the overpasses, guardrails, curbs, and attending structures. Instead of being constructed with the outside corners of the concrete meeting at right angles, and being very boxy, like those here in America, they met at seventy-five- or eighty-degree angles and had a much more natural look. The roads were asphalt and well maintained. There was not as much effort placed into prettying-up the throughway, as there is in America, but the trees I could see were different. I noticed them right off, they were mainly eucalyptus, with a few pine and elm trees interspersed.

As we were driving on the throughway, I asked Anna about the trees and their differences. She explained that the eucalyptus were native to Australia and were more abundant in the lower elevations. The pines and elms were originally imported many years ago, and grow more abundantly in the higher elevations.

As we exited the throughway and approached Melbourne proper, Anna pointed out different landmarks and told me a little bit about the city. We drove into town and through a business district that could have been a typical main street in any American small-town. As we traveled, we entered an area that became more suburban, and the streets were empty of traffic. Traveling into the suburbs, I noticed that the houses were modest yet comfortably decorated and obviously built to last. The one big difference between Australian big cities and the major cities in America such as my hometown, Los Angeles, is the cleanliness in Australia. The vegetation, also, was plentiful and green. We were heading to a house where she was house-sitting. The owners were away on vacation in Europe. We would have the house to ourselves she told me, which suited me just fine.

We arrived at a small, two-story, brick house a couple of doors in from the corner, on a narrow road. She pulled into the driveway next door to let me out. After I got out, and out of the way, she pulled the car up into the space in front of the garage of the house. There were no curbs in this neighborhood. This would become our mode of coming and going.

We went around the side of the house, through a gate, down a walkway, plush with bushes and vegetation that I did not readily recognize, and down a step into the backyard. The backyard was relatively small, surrounded by wood fencing, with vines growing over a portion of the fencing. It consisted of two levels. The lower level was covered with bricks, and had a small, round, faded red and weather-worn picnic table in the middle. On one side of brick patio, a wall of brick rose about eighteen inches to the upper level, which had a nicer table with chairs under a wood-slatted overhang in the yard. She unlocked a sliding glass door that entered into the back of the house. She told me that she did not really have to lock the house, but after having traveled in America, she now felt safer locking the door wherever she went.

The first room we entered was about twelve feet square, divided by an island that separated the dining room from the kitchen. The eating area had dark walls. To the right of the door was a small cabinet with sliding doors in the front, mounted on four tapered round legs. Balanced on top of the cabinet was a large boom box that played mellow rock, which I thought sounded like rock-and-roll from America. I didn't inquire about the music though. That would come later. Close by, a second cabinet was mounted to the wall about two feet from the floor and reached to the ceiling, which was probably about ten feet high. Across from the cabinet were a small table and chairs and in the back corner was a beanbag chair poised beneath more wall shelves filled with knickknacks.

Anna had constructed a ramp of sorts out of plywood that covered the stairs and lead toward a hallway leading to the back of the house. The ramp was quite steep and Anna needed to help me up it. She showed me to a room at the far end of the hallway. It was sparsely furnished with nothing more than two beds. One of the beds was piled with extra bedding and blankets. I unloaded my bags and began to settle in.

When I came out of the room I saw through the door to the right an enclosed bathtub and shower.

Upon entering, I also found a cabinet with a sink built in, but no toilet. This seemed strange, so I backed out and proceeded down the hallway to the kitchen. Before I got there, I noticed another door, which was ajar, and when I looked in, I saw just a toilet. This surprised me, and scratching my head I went on down the hall to the top of the ramp.

"What's with the toilet being in a separate room by itself from the bathroom?" I asked her inquiringly. "The toilet is supposed to be in the bathroom, isn't it?"

She looked up, startled from what she was looking at on the table, almost as if she had forgotten I was there in the house. What she had been reading looked to be some brochures and maps.

"Oh," she said, laughing to herself, "in Australia the toilet, what we call 'the Lu', is, like in England, separate from the what we call the 'Bathing Room.'" She was smiling now, but burst out laughing when she saw the perplexed look on my face.

"Here in Australia we follow many of the customs of England. After all, Australia was formerly a British colony. I suppose that's the reason the lu, or toilet, is separate. In the old days, before modern plumbing, people didn't want to bathe or wash up in a room that smelled like an outhouse. Besides, the outhouse was just that, outside the house. You'll find that many things here in Australia are based on British customs.

Anna got up, climbed up the ramp, with some difficulty of her own, and helped me down the ramp. I got a closer look at what she had been looking over at the table. They were travel brochures of Melbourne and the surrounding areas: Sydney, Cairns, Brisbane, Adelaide, Perth, Alice Springs and Darwin. She also had several maps and some basic literature about Australia. She had collected these so I wouldn't feel so out of sorts when I arrived. She was very well organized and thoughtful in tha you t way.

I had also brought my own collection of brochures and maps. After explaining to her that they were in one of my bags in the room, she went to receive them and bring them out. I pulled up to the table and started going through her brochures and the ones I had brought. Just seeing the names of different cities that were now within reach was exciting: Melbourne, Sydney, Brisbane and Alice Springs. I oriented myself by looking over the large map of the entire continent. I had a brochure on Perth, but I was fairly certain I would never get to go there. It was on the other side of the continent, almost three thousand miles away. She had several more brochures, containing information on different local constabularies in the surrounding cities as well as brochures on Perth, Adelaide, Darwin and more. For the next few hours, we sat talking, laughing and discussing our possible plans.

I sat looking then, finally reading the information in front of me. The more I read, the more unsettled I became. There was so much information, and I realized I had not thought much beyond just getting to Australia. And now here I was with no plan beyond the fact that I had a place to stay for the night, and the company of a friend. So without putting too much emphasis on what we did, I suggested that we take it one day at a time. Decide on what we were going to do tomorrow and leave it at that.

I asked her what she did for work and she said she was between positions as a Play Therapist. I was familiar with the term, what I wanted to hear her explain it in her own words.

"I work with children in a hospital doing Play Therapy. My work involves playing with the children just after surgery or a trauma to help them find solutions to the problems that might affect their lives, now or in the future. Play Therapy is part of Sand Play Therapy that was developed by Dora Kalff, a Swiss psychologist and close collaborator of C.G. Jung, a world-renowned psychoanalyst. It has been widely used in many parts of this country and throughout the world," she explained. "It's kind of a textbook type of answer, but I found over the years that many people do not understand what Play Therapy is. So, I came up with this wordy explanation in order for people to understand. I studied this when I was living in Ontario and got a position in a local hospital. I love my work."

I got the impression that she did not want to talk very much about her job situation, other than saying she was sending an inquiry letter to another hospital and she felt certain that they would hire her. I let the conversation about her work drop at this point.

There were, of course, many things Anna wanted to do and places she wanted to go. She kept saying that because she was in between jobs, my coming to visit at this time would allow her an opportunity to do her own exploring while taking me around the city.

"It's great that you could come to Australia and I am very honored that you chose me to be the one you came to visit," she said.

"I am so glad I met you back in the states in Tucson. And I am so glad we kept in touch since we met. You know from my letters that I have always wanted to come to Australia. You helped give me the courage to make this dream come true," I said.

"I get a chance to see my own city in a different light and it's fun to look at everything as though I am seeing it for the first time. When someone visits I look at things that I've taken for granted for years and have told myself that 'one day I will stop and see that,' but never do. So I am glad you came," she said cheerfully and suggested we go get a pizza.

"Pizza!? Where can we get a pizza? Do you really have pizza?" I asked almost dumbfounded.

"Yes of course we have pizza," she said laughing. “Australia is not as backwards as you may think it is."

"Well . . . I didn't know." I replied. "So, where is this pizza parlor?"

"Just a few blocks away. We can walk over there," she said.

Grabbing our coats and locking up we began moving toward the nearby pizza parlor. The houses in the neighborhood looked like any other neighborhood in any other city. The big difference though was that the cars along the curb, in either direction, were parked facing the opposite direction. And when approaching someone on the sidewalk, I would be walking on the right side of the sidewalk, as in America, and people walking towards us would be walking on the left side of the sidewalk, as is the custom of Australia, and I would wind up doing a two-step to get out the way of on-coming pedestrians. Anna seemed to enjoy my disorientation, since it made her laugh.

"We pass each other on the left instead of the right," she said pointing out my difficulty.

"On which side do you have dogs walk?" I asked. I didn't know why that came to mind, but it may have been the fact that just before I left for Australia I applied for a service dog and was put on a waiting list. One of the things I remembered, subconsciously, was that they teach the dog to heel on the left.

"Dogs usually walk on their owner's right," she answered, stopping and looking a little perplexed. I explained about the service dog school that I had applied to and their teaching method. With my explanation, she understood and we continued toward the pizza parlor.

When we arrived Anna held the door and we both entered to a quiet wood paneled and sectioned room about a quarter filled with customers. The place had the same feeling as any other pizza parlor, right down to the customary sawdust on the floor. We ordered a pizza with half vegetarian and half pepperoni. Anna was vegetarian. The pepperoni tasted a little different than I was accustomed to--more like roast beef. Anna ordered a soft drink and I ordered a beer. I started to order Foster's Lager, after all, in the US "Foster's, is Australian for beer," as Paul Hogan made the line famous in the Foster's Lager commercial. But Anna stopped me saying that "Foster's" was not "the beer" that most people preferred in Australia. Most people drink "Piss" beer. I thought what an odd name. Who would want to drink a beer named Piss? It's what we do when we go to the bathroom. I wondered at this for a time, but then I thought I would relent and I considered her recommendation, and against my better judgment, decided to order it. To my relief, I was quite surprised how good it was. When we were finished, we quietly slipped out and made our way back to the house..

We talked into the early hours of the following morning. She explained a few of the expressions and sayings of the Australian dialect. In Australia, they speak English, more with a British flavor than American flavor, but many of the expressions are unique to Australia, and some are not.

"This is 'the box'," she said, pointing to the TV. "It's named after the tele-communications box, I think. It's also called 'the tele,' but I prefer just calling it 'the box.'"

"And this is just called 'tunes'", she said, pointing to the radio.

"And then there is the cute little phrase 'two shakes of a lamb's tail,' which means to hurry or to do something very quickly." This term gave me a good laugh. I could just picture two old farmer's on the back forty surrounded by sheep and zipping up their pants. I shook this vision out of my head and came back to the room. I had never heard this term and thought it quite endearing.

"The culture of Australia in itself is a combination of English and Irish, to begin with. Australia originally was an English colony formed by convicts back in the 1800's. Now, it still has a lot of English and Irish, but also a multitude of other cultural influences and is very Americanized. "Though you'd be loath to say that to most Australians," Anna said. "Australians are a proud, and somewhat arrogant, people who feel that Australia and Australians are a totally separate line, all its own."

"Many of the television shows and movies are American, with very few Australian-based shows," she continued. "The music on many of the radio stations is also American, but ten or so years behind American radio and only playing what you in America consider soft rock."

"There are several Australian bands that are getting air-play and are becoming quite popular in the states," I told her. "Men at Work, for instance, and Midnight Oil, of which I have several albums."

"Yes they are getting quite popular here also. Midnight Oil, I mean," she said.

We ended the evening by agreeing that we'd begin the next day at 6:00 a.m., with a trip to a koala sanctuary about forty miles out of Melbourne. I was looking forward to a chance to learn more at this zoological exhibit.

The storm was getting worse. Periodically the overhead speakers would crackle to life and the captain would briefly announce in a muffled voice that the storm was increasing in intensity, assuring us all the while that there was nothing to worry about. The sound was scratchy and it was hard to make out. Suddenly a bolt of lightning shattered one of the windows in the mid-section of the plane, a few rows in front of me. At the same time, there was a blinding flash of pure white light filling the cabin. The plane lost no altitude and the air did not go rushing out the open window, as I'd witnessed in movies. I glanced at my watch to note the time and I noticed that the face was different, and it took a few seconds to realize that the numbers had been flipped and the second hand was turning counter-clockwise. Finally, the plane was no longer passing through a storm, and I could see out the windows that the sky was clear, a beautiful blue, with cotton-like white clouds. The flight attendants seemed translucent as they passed ghost-like up and down the aisles. They no longer seemed upset by the storm, or lack thereof, which I knew had ended as abruptly as it had started. I reached up to put on the call light to find out what was happening and at the same time I felt a touch on my shoulder and looked up . . . .it was Anna! How had she gotten on the plane?

The touch became more of a shake, and groggily it dawned on me that I was dreaming. I lay there blinking and rubbing my eyes. It was too early. I had just closed my eyes. Anna kept shaking me until she was sure that I was awake.

"God, what time is it?" I sounded hoarse, as if I had gravel in my throat.

"It's six o'clock. We agreed last night to start out early this morning." She cheerfully said.

I mumbled a reply, climbed out from under the covers, and she helped me into my chair and pushed me down the hallway and then the ramp. I said I wanted a cigarette, and she pointed to the table outside to where an ashtray sat on the round picnic table. I made my way to the table outside, struggling over the threshold, where I lit a cigarette and brushed out my long hair. I was all but naked, except for a towel draped across my lap. She brought out breakfast, which consisted of homemade muffins and coffee. She had made the muffins herself. They were a combination of bran and blueberry, and were quite good. The coffee, on the other hand, was God-awful strong, and I asked her about this.

"It's instant coffee made with three heaping tablespoons per cup; isn't it good ?" She explained with obvious sincerity.

"I like strong coffee, but it's more like coffee flavored syrup," I said, and noticing the crestfallen look on her face, I quickly added. "You know this ain't half bad." Her cheerful smile quickly returned.

She looked at me thoughtfully for a moment, as if she was debating whether to say something to me. Finally she just gave up her inward unresolved debate and asked.

"I couldn't help but notice that you had that little stuffed dog with you in bed. I recognized it from the seminar where we met. That counselor, what was her name, gave it to you during one of the sessions, I remember that," she said, still looking a little sheepish about even broaching the subject. I suspected she was afraid she was delving into an area of intimacy that would embarrass me.

"You saw that, did you?" I smiled, attempting to disarm her fear that she may have offended me. And then I laughed.

"It is kind of childish, I know, to sleep with a stuffed animal, but I started the practice after I had to put my dog down," I explained.

"I had that dog for eight years, ever since he was a puppy. He was an ugly old Pit-bull named 'Shotgun.' I had to put him down, because he had "snapped." His problems started when he had eaten some fur off an old set of antlers from a deer that had been mounted and he got sick. This was back when he was about two months old. He almost died. As a result, he got worms that ate up his insides and traveled into his brain. The vet said this might happen. One day he didn't recognize me and started to attack me. I loved and hated that dog. Well, after I had put him down, I felt kind of uneasy around the house without him. It wasn't that he was trained, in fact, he barely had any training at all, but having him around just made me feel much safer," Just talking about him made me feel sad, but I continued. "Thinking of him always brings back good memories. He was the only dog I knew that would curl his lip whenever he smelled something with a bad odor. But there were also a lot of shitty memories. He was a real pain in the butt. There were also times . . . Well I could go on talking about him, but we would be here all day."

"Anyway after he died I saw the little stuffed dog sitting on a shelf in the corner of my room. I had forgotten that I had him. I thought, 'this ugly little dog reminds me of Shotgun, although he is a completely different color.' I picked him up and I don't know what told me to take it to bed, but I did. I felt much safer and more at ease and he became part of my bedroom routine," I explained.

"Well," I said, looking at my watch, which I had not taken off the night before, and noticed the time. "If I go on talking we will be here all day. Sometimes, I get to talking and forget the time."

We had finished our breakfast. "Let's get going," I said.

"You'd make a great scene, dressed like that," she said smiling and pointing to my naked body.

I looked down and laughed. She pushed me up the ramp where I quickly got dressed.

Climbing into the car we headed toward the sanctuary. The city seemed to breathe in life and the air was fresh and clean, with a crispness that comes only after a rain. I asked her about this and she said that it had rained last night. I had dreamily slept through it.

We arrived at the sanctuary, which I kept referring to as a "zoo," and Anna kept correcting me. On the outside of the sanctuary in the parking lot was a coffee establishment. Both Anna and I wanted another cup of "real" coffee, and she went in to get us some, but before she went in she asked me if I wanted it "white" or "sweet." I had no idea what she was saying.

"What? What do you mean by white or sweet?" I asked, looking at her nonplussed.

"Oh, yeah. I forgot you don't know our customs. In Australia we either drink our coffee with cream, which is what we call 'white,' or with cream and sugar, which is what we call 'sweet,'" she explained.

"Sweet? White? I just like black coffee," I said, thinking that their terms for coffee were a bit narrow.

"Oh! You want Yank coffee," she smiled. "Yeah, I like it that way too, sometimes. A lot of places, if you just ask for, 'Yank' coffee, they know to serve the coffee just black. It's one of those unsaid social rules," she added as we took a few minutes to drink our coffee.

Soon after, the gates to the sanctuary were opened for the day. We were the first and only people there. The long winding path took us past many exhibits. When we reached the Tasmanian Devil exhibit, I was very surprised. The animal was so small. Not much bigger than a small pig. About ten or eleven inches in height. It was shaped much like a pig, except that the face more closely resembled that of a very small bear. It was covered with thick, coarse, black fur. I always had envisioned the Tasmanian Devil as a big and burly animal, like in the Warner Brothers cartoons. It just goes to show how TV can influence our perceptions of reality.

Another exhibit that really fascinated me was the tree-kangaroo. The actual name was the Lumholtz Tree-Kangaroo. Tree-kangaroos spend most of their time in trees, so their limbs are different from the standard kangaroos I had seen in photographs. Their front and back limbs are more equal in length. Their forearms are longer and stronger. I found out that there were in fact dozens, if not more, different strains of kangaroos in Australia. I looked up into the tree and there, in fact unmistakably, was a kangaroo.

As we continued on the path we went through a double gate made of chain-link fencing, into an open courtyard. The path cut across the courtyard diagonally on a land bridge, about a meter above the ground. Off to one side of the path stood a lone, stunted eucalyptus tree bearing few leaves. In one of the crooks formed by a branch growing from the trunk, sat a koala, dozing lazily in the sun. This evidently was the main attraction, hence the reason for the name "The Koala Reserve." It appeared to be the lone occupant of the exhibit, because, looking around, I saw no others. Stopping, I read the sign attached to the fence directly across from the lone tree. I was surprised to learn that koalas sleep during most of the day, and move around and to feed at night. They are territorial animals. They do not wander aimlessly through the bush. Koalas only eat leaves from the eucalyptus. They are virtually addicted to this plant. The koala receives only about twelve percent of its nutrients from this plant, and that is why it moves so slowly, barely having the energy to hang on and keep feeding. Periodically koalas are found on the ground with broken limbs, having lost their grip and tumbled thirty or more feet to the ground.

Having done the complete circuitous path of the sanctuary, we were back at the main gate. Reluctantly we climbed back in the car and headed out. Driving home, I began to imagine I was truly an Australian and that the house we were staying in was home.

Anna aimed the car in a different direction this time, traveling down an isolated highway quite different from the way we had come. I had no idea where we were.

Suddenly, Anna turned to me and asked, "Do you want to stop at the winery?"

"Winery . . .?" I queried, turning towards her. I swung my head around in all directions. The only thing for miles around that I could see were fields of cabbage-like-looking plants, which, upon closer inspection I recognized as grape vines. I realized I had not been paying all that much attention to the fields around us. The road we were on was right in the middle of a grape orchard. We had not passed another car in about half an hour. I turned to her with a bewildered expression on my face. She looked at me and burst out laughing.

“I take that, as a yes," she said and proceeded to turn down another, even more isolated, highway.

As she drove, I didn't see anything except more grape orchards. Beginning to think that Anna had been mistaken in her recollection of there being a winery on this road, we came across a shack, not more than about four or five meters square, and painted off-white. It had an overhanging, slant roof on one side covering a small concrete patio. Surprisingly, a dozen or so cars were parked outside this structure in the middle of nowhere.

As we drove up I could see people were entering the structure, and when they came out it appeared as if they had glasses in their hands. Some people were sitting on their cars in the bright hot sun, but most were standing in what little shade the overhanging roof provided.

Anna proceeded to enter the building as I climbed out of the car. She came out with two glasses of wine. Under the overhang a few people shuffled and managed to make room for Anna and I to sit in the shade. We finished our glasses of wine and Anna went inside again and came out with more wine. Surprised, because I thought she was going in to return the glasses, I laughed heartily and we continued talking.

"This is a hell of a place for a wine tasting establishment," I said to Anna. "What is it doing out in the middle of nowhere?"

"It's part of the orchard," she replied. "All of the larger orchards around here have these wineries for people to taste their wine. People tend to buy more wine after they have had a few glasses."

"Still, where 's the signs, where's the advertising?" I asked, shaking my head.

"They don't want to advertise this place. If they advertised the winery there would be fifty or so cars parked around here and that could lead to fights and all sorts of things," she said..

Several more times she went back in to replenish

our glasses, and the final time she stayed inside for several minutes. When she came out she held a bottle of port, citing her need for something to relax her on the nights when she had trouble sleeping. I'm sure she purchased the bottle of wine because she felt a little guilty for both of us having had more than our share of free spirits. As we left I was feeling no pain and I am not quite certain how we made it home.

The next morning I noticed that both rods that hold my foot plates were bent. When I reached over to try to straighten one of the rods, it broke off in my hands. Well hell, I thought to myself. I reached over to determine the security of the other one, it was not broken, but bent enough that it would need to be repaired. I assumed I'd have to find a machine shop to have the rods welded. But the more I considered my situation, the more I was convinced I could figure out another way to resolve my problem. It occurred to me that if I kept my feet off the ground, I could function just fine. My wheelchair was made in such a way that I found by attaching a strap to the clamps that hold the rods for my foot plates, across the front and from each side, it would stabilize my feet. With this idea in hand I then dismounted the bent rod and attached the strap. It changed the balance of the chair so it was easier to tilt backwards, and it also altered the way I maneuvered, but none of this seemed critical to my safety. This was a makeshift solution, but it sufficed. I was not about to let this obstacle, which was more of an inconvenience than anything else, stop me. I had already made it this far, and I was not to be defeated by this small challenge.

The following week I spent in Melbourne, taking in as many sites as I possibly could. One evening we went to a street festival. Several blocks of the downtown area had been cordoned off with booths selling everything from music, food, and handcrafted jewelry to Aboriginal art. Several bands played to a dancing crowd. When we arrived a band was playing reggae music. A band playing rock-and-roll followed, with several cutting renditions of Midnight Oil tunes. For a finale, the last band of the evening consisted of traditional Australian instruments playing a variety of Aboriginal music.

"What is the long log-shaped instrument that man is playing?" I asked Anna.

"A didgeridoo," she replied.

"A what?"

"A didgeridoo. It's an instrument made by the Aborigines and played originally in their Dream Time ceremonies," Anna explained.

The sound of a didgeridoo is unique. I had never heard it before. It produces a low deep, gruff, hollow sound that resonates. It was unlike any instrument I had ever heard.

Talking about this instrument brought to mind how I had read when I was a boy about the Aboriginal culture and how I found it to be fascinating.

Their myths , stories, beliefs about the creation of Australia as well as their myriads of rituals and ceremonies fascinated me. Dreamtime stories filled my imagination, especially when they described a trance-like state where time becomes meaningless and the characters travel through time and place to an ancestral plane of existence. They hear conversations, follow paths that have been traveled, view scenes and people, that had taken place years before, and their understanding of Dreamtime is that it is as real, or even more so, than the present and the conscious world. Some of my understanding seemed incomplete and so I wanted to find out a little bit more. And so Anna took me to a museum full of displays and descriptions of the Australian Aboriginal culture.

In the Dandenong Ranges, just outside of Melbourne, about thirty minutes away, was the William Ricketts Sanctuary. It is a place of beauty and tranquility, featuring many sculptures and carvings, at least eighty-six in all, sculpted out of clay, stone and wood by William Ricketts, in his ninety years plus. Due to both the natural setting and the mystical sculptures, half hidden among ferns along the pathways, I found it to be a perfect place for quiet reflection and for contemplating the essence of the vision of William Ricketts. Some of the sculptures were intricately carved whereas others were quite simple. I was so taken with the beauty and wonder of this place that I had a picture taken of me with one of the sculptures.

Another evening during the week I contacted the woman I had met in the airport in Los Angeles, Rosemary, who lived in Brighton and who had invited me to visit her and her family. She and her husband, Hedley, picked me up an hour later. Driving back to their house they took me by way of the Melbourne harbor, which is north and East of the city about five minutes.

As we entered the harbor, Hedley pulled into a lot next to a tall wooden structure. I was somewhat perplexed, but as we neared it, I noticed it was open on one side. Turning the corner in the car, I saw it was filled with boats. I was simply amazed. I was looking at boats stacked five or six high and three across, on shelves, or slips, similar to those you'd find on boat trailers. Hedley pointed to a boat second from the top in the center row and exclaimed that was his boat. All I could realistically see was that it was a dual inboard, which looked about the size of a cabin cruiser. I don't know know boats very well, but I noticed that across the aft, I think that is what it is called, in large, script-like, letters was stenciled out the name of the boat, "Rosemary." I complemented him on having a nice boat. It was a nice boat -- and least what I could see of it.

I began looking around the harbor and I noticed that there were several more structures just like this one. Fascinated, I asked why the boats were housed in this fashion. They said that it was because Melbourne harbor was small and this way the harbor could hold many more boats. They would just call in the morning and the people at the harbor would forklift the boat out of its slot in the structure and put it in the water, mooring it to one of the several docks, awaiting their arrival.

This was all explained to me as we drove back into the city. Along the way back to their home, we stopped at a drive through market, the kind that used to be popular back in the states many years ago. What surprised me was that Hedley purchased a bottle of wine in this outdoor market. Back in California, alcoholic beverages are sold only in liquor stores or supermarkets.

The further we drove into the heart of the city, the nicer the neighborhoods became. The houses got larger and the yards were better maintained. My hosts were apparently well off. We pulled into the driveway of a two-story house with a carefully tended cactus garden in the front. The entryway was covered. and I saw as we entered that it opened out into the dining area. Beyond that was a sunken living room, which looked out through sliding glass doors, onto the backyard. The dining area had a high ceiling, which was open to a hallway leading crosswise to the upper story of the house. I presumed that this hallway lead to bedrooms on either side. The kitchen was off to the side of the dining area, with a low counter that looked into the dining area and the living room.

I was introduced to their three sons John, Hedley

and Matthew, about thirteen, fourteen and sixteen. While Rosemary prepared dinner, we talked about what I had and seen so far and what I thought of Australia.

"Riding in a car traveling on the other side of the road is very disorienting" I told them. "I just get used to traveling on the wrong side of the road, to me it's the wrong side, and you turn the corner and it feels like you are turning into the wrong side again, into what feels like it's going to be oncoming traffic," I said.

Rosemary laughed and said that it was a hard for her also when she first came to Australia.

"Anna was telling me about the name of the beer that you drink here in Australia, or at least in Victoria, Australia. It's called 'Piss'," I said, laughing. "What a name," I told her, again laughing, "that's what you do when you go to the bathroom."

"Yes," she said. "I suppose it is. I don't know the whole story behind the name. Just that it's good beer."

"Anna and I went to a street festival last night and there were several bands. The last one had an instrument that I had never seen or heard before, a didgeridoo. The sound was unique. A low, haunting, drone. I liked it a lot. Anna was telling me that they blow into it."

"Yes, but I have never been able to play it. Many white people can't play it. It seems to be a very native thing," she explained.

Being a mother, she talked a lot about how life was in Australia for her boys. At one point in the conversation she mentioned how her sons had to go through dreary summer vacations. They were out of school for three months for school break, which is June through September, and because school break is during their winter (Australia is in the southern hemisphere and the seasons are reversed) it is cold and rainy and often overcast. I asked her why the government hadn't seen to it to change the school schedule to suit the southern hemisphere time zone. She just shook her head and shrugged.

Dinner was stuffed crab and steamed vegetables. It was quite good. After dinner, we sat around the table and I noticed a clock on the wall. I looked at it and then at my watch and could see that it was probably stopped, because the time was wrong. I then noticed that the second hand was moving and I checked my watch again. Rosemary saw me looking at the wall and then at my watch, and turned to see what I was looking at. Chuckling to herself, she got up and took the clock down, bringing it over to where we were sitting.

"It's a joke clock," she said, showing it to me. "The reason you were probably confused when you were looking at it is because it's backwards."

I could then see that she was correct. It was indeed backwards. All the numbers were interposed. The 10 being where the 2 would be on a regular clock and the same with all the other numbers. The hands moved backwards, or counterclockwise. I got quite a kick out of the clock.

We talked long into the night, and finally I mentioned that I should get back to Anna's, asking if one of them could drive me back.

"Nonsense," Rosemary said, "we'll just call Anna and you can stay here. We have plenty of room. You can stay in our guest room."

The following morning I thanked my hosts for an enjoyable visit, before Anna, joined by her sister, Mary, picked me up. Anna said we were going to an island off the south-eastern tip of Australia, about 200 miles from Melbourne. The island was called Philip Island.

Philip Island is more of a peninsula off the coast of Australia than an actual island. We did drive across a short bridge, which I suppose is why they call it an island. As we drove down the main street, Anna pointed out the different sites along the way, including a building that Anna said was a clock museum.

I had had a fascination for time and time pieces for most of my life so I suggested that we stop. Like those of many of the buildings on the island, the entrance was raised off the ground with about a dozen wooden steps. The building itself was on stilts. Both Anna and her sister pulled me up the steps, one on each side. Once inside we found that it was a house with several rooms filled with different clocks. Some were old and rare. Some were contemporary.

We even came across a clock similar to the clock in Rosemary's house and it suddenly occurred to me that it was also similar to the watch in my dream.

This clock held a special fascination for me. It seemed to have the ability to play tricks with my deeply-rooted concept of time. I loved the idea and realized it was for sale. I decided to buy it. I noted the price of seventy-five dollars and thought this was a bit much for a joke. Besides, the establishment was probably stacking the price because the museum is a tourist attraction. I offered fifty dollars. I was immediately turned down, so I turned away to begin to look at T-shirts. After a few minutes, the sales lady approached me and said that the owner was willing to make an exception and accept my offer. I left the museum with a prize possession that is jokingly called, "The Down Under Clock." I also purchased a shirt with a picture of a kangaroo on a very simple landscape contrasted against a clear blue sky and a beaming sun. The words scribed across the top of the picture was "Walkabout Australia."

It was getting on towards mid-afternoon and we were getting hungry. We stopped at a snack bar that was up on a hill, in the back of an open dirt lot overlooking a cliff. The cliff was along the ocean side off the straits between Australia and Tasmania. The bitter cold of the wind felt as though it was blowing off the ice flows of Antarctica. It whipped through my indecently thin Levi jacket and made me wish I had brought a heavier coat. The wind stung my bare cheeks and stopped me dead in my tracks. If it had been blowing the opposite direction I could have spread my jacket and the wind would have carried me across the lot to the snack bar. With Anna's help, I was able to make my way there.

Once we were at the snack bar it became apparent that my wheelchair would not fit through the doorway. I was stuck huddling in the bitter cold behind a siding of the building designed to break the wind. This was nothing more than a piece of plywood. Anna and her sister went in to escape the cold and to get something to eat. When they came out, we headed back to the car. There was no way we were going to sit at the picnic tables that were erected just outside the snack bar. In the car, we ate and Anna explained about the penguin exhibit, where we were going next.

"The penguin exhibit," she explained, "is a place to watch the 'Penguin Parade.'"

She went on to explain that it was the annual migration of both the “mother and father” penguins coming ashore at dusk to feed the young offspring they had abandoned at daybreak to feed. The chicks are tucked safely into their hidden nests nestled within the vegetation along the beach. The adults go out to sea to feed during the day. At dusk, they return to their young and regurgitate their daily feeding. We humans have taken it upon ourselves to find this both endearing and fascinating. The people of Philip Island saw this as an opportunity to make money. Building bleachers and walkways, or land bridges, leading to the bleachers looking out onto the water, they began charging the public to see this unique event.

We found a place to park, paid the entrance fee and headed onto the wooden walkways to the bleachers, which were made of cement. The first seat was down a step, so there was no way I could transfer to the bleachers. We decided to claim an area on one of the wooden walkways. No sooner had we done this than a hoard of Japanese tourists flooded forward, trying to get between the guardrail and myself. Anna and her sister blocked the way on either side of us. Anna explained that the Japanese had a different sense of personal space. Theirs is much smaller than that of most Westerners.

The sun began to set in the gray, overcast, stormy sky, and no sooner had the light begun to fade than the first of the "adult" penguins made their way hesitantly and cautiously ashore. Waddling with their daily feeding and often falling forward from the weight, it was quite a spectacle to see them as they made their way unerringly up the many paths through the sand and tufts of vegetation to the nests. Their young chirped loudly, encouraging them on. I thought it amazing that these penguins knew, out of the hundreds of singing chirps, which was their young.

I read later that penguins normally have only one offspring, and either instinctively know where the nest is or can distinctly separate the sounds of their offspring from the hundreds of chirps. It is probably like our hearing a distinct voice out of a crowd, yet, in a foreign language all the voices sound the same.

5

Sydney - A Visit From the Turban King

After four or five days in Melbourne, I ended up taking a bus to Sydney. My initial plan was to take the train, but due to unanticipated delays at the railroad station, I missed my scheduled departure. The circumstances around the delays were amusing to me, but not to Anna.

We had scheduled to leave the house about 10 o'clock in the morning, but Anna could not find her keys. Looking upstairs through all her belongings and downstairs through all my belongings, the kitchen, the living room, the dining area twice, we finally found them laying behind the ashtray on the picnic table outside. She had laid them down when she joined me outside that morning when I had smoked a cigarette. It was about 10:30 before we finally headed towards the train station. Anna had called ahead to find out the train schedule and the train was to leave at 11:15. The station was about thirty minutes from the house. We were going to cut it close.

We made it to the train station and purchased my ticket. My luggage went directly from the ticket counter and had gotten aboard. While waiting for my boarding announcement, I felt the need to use the restroom.

"Where's the handicapped restroom?" I asked one of the station hands.

"There is no handicapped restroom," he replied. After pausing a minute he added, "There is a rest-room that would accommodate your wheelchair down on the lower level. Take this walkway down to that service elevator over there," he pointed, "and take it to level B. It's only down a few steps, but I don't think that you can get down there in your wheelchair."

We took the rickety old service elevator down and the restroom was clearly marked, but was down a cluttered hallway. We made our way around each obstacle and finally made it to the restroom. It took longer than expected, because I was having trouble with my leg bag.

"It took, 'three shakes of a lamb's tail'" I said to Anna as I exited the restroom chuckling to myself, thinking that this was a clever turn of the phrase 'two shakes of a lamb's tail.' But Anna just smiled. I don't think she found it all that funny.

By the time we wound our way back through the clutter and up the elevator to the platform the train had left without me. My abandoned luggage had been placed on the platform next to the empty rails.

Anna was furious. We went to the Station Master. Anna screamed at him, "How could you let the train leave?"

"I didn't know where you were," the Station Master said.

"How could you not," replied Anna in an irritated voice, "you sent us to that restroom." And then thinking, she said, "You know what I think. I think you knew that we wouldn't make it back in time." She shook with fury. "I think, you owe this man a trip to Sydney. He has a tour scheduled for early tomorrow."

"There are no more trains scheduled to leave for Sydney for two days," the Station Master said. "He will miss the tour."

"Put up the money for a bus then," Anna said.

The Station Master scowled and mumbled something unintelligible, but finally, and with obvious reluctance, agreed. We walked with him and to the interior of the station to his office where he grabbed a binder off of the shelf and doggedly fumbled through his list of numbers and called a bus station and made a reservation for me.

I was somewhat bewildered by the whole exchange because I got the vague impression that Anna wanted me to leave. Why, I didn't know. The bewildering part was, Anna had arranged to meet me in Sydney at the end of the week.

Arriving in Sydney I took a taxi from the bus station to a hotel, where I would be picked up for the tour the next day. It was located on the other side of Sydney. The taxi ride took about forty-five minutes. Arrangements had been made for me to be picked up early in the morning to go on a tour to the Kakadoo Mountains. The tour was put together by a disabled tourist organization. It had been the only tour I scheduled myself during this trip, and even though it was advertised as being completely accessible, it was still against my "independent principles" to sign on. I had some vague notion that a tour was confining and compromising, and I knew that I would want to stay at a particular place far longer than the tour would allow. In addition I hate, with a deep-down-passion, to be rushed. The hotel was on the far side of Sydney and I figured that because I was to be picked up at an early hour, from the hotel, I might as well stay there for the night, I paid the sobering price of one-hundred-seventy-nine dollars for one night. It was far more than I had ever paid to stay at any other place, in Australia or anywhere else in my life. It broke my heart to part with so much money, just for a bed.

That night just as I was transferring to bed, a knock came at the door. It startled me. I lost my concentration and wound up on the floor between the bed and my wheelchair. I called out to whoever had knocked.

"Mr. Fritz, the tour has been canceled because of equipment failure," came the reply of a woman, through the door.

Not thinking quickly enough, I failed to ask when it was going to be rescheduled. The woman left and I didn't call the tour office because, I reasoned, that, maybe I wasn't supposed to be on that tour in the first place. I didn't even feel disappointed, because the thought of being tied down, literally and figuratively, really never appealed to me in the first place. Besides, having no schedule was part of the adventure.

The following morning, after having a pleasant breakfast at the hotel, which in Australia is not a regular custom, I took a taxi back across Sydney, to the coastal side. I did not know where I would stay, but I had a brochure and a map of all the youth hostels in Australia. I picked one out and arranged for a room.

When I arrived at the hostel, I discovered the room was up a flight of stairs on the mezzanine level. I decided to skip going to the room right then and chose to go the few miles down to the harbor. The journey was rather difficult, and dangerous at times, because I had to go through a narrow tunnel against traffic and around a blind turn for part of the way. A couple of hours later I arrived at the Sydney Harbor Mall.

I spent the next several hours perusing the mall. It was a typical mall for the most part, but in some ways it was unique. It had much more handcrafted local pieces. I stopped at one point to have a hand-drawn portrait done of me, with my mid-back-length hair and belly-button-length beard. That would be for my mother, I decided.

After going up and down the mall for several hours, I grew tired of exploring the different stores. Because the trip back to the hostel would be mainly up hill, I decided to take a taxi. Easier said than done.

"No. I cannot take you in the taxi. There is no place to put your wheelchair," the man, of middle-Eastern descent, insisted.

"You can put my wheelchair in the trunk, and then take it out when we get there," I said, explaining and pantomiming the procedure of folding and unfolding my wheelchair.

"But who is going to help you get in the car?"

"I will get in the car myself," I exclaimed. "And then I will get back into my wheelchair when we get there."

"No . . . I cannot take you ."

I hassled with several taxi drivers. They all had the same or similar arguments. It seemed ridiculous to me, but then I was not the one lifting my chair in an out of the trunk. Finally, I managed to get a ride back to the youth hostel. It seems that many of the taxi drivers were foreign to Australia and had never had a passenger in a wheelchair and were confused as to how to manage with someone like me in their taxi.

At the youth hostel, I had no trouble getting someone to pull me up the stairs to my room. It turned out that my room was a private room with two beds and a private bath.

The next day, I had “breakfast” in the hostel bistro, which adjoined the living area, down another flight of steps. I did not enjoy the hassle of staying in a room, however private it was, on a different level from the bistro and living area, and then there were the stairs to the street. I checked out and walked two-and-one-half kilometers to another hostel on my list. This was not any better, because the kitchen and laundry facilities were both down a steep flight of stairs. At least the toilet and showers were on the same level as the room, though. Because the list did not specify any other youth hostels in that portion of Sydney, I decided to stay there.

Anna arrived as scheduled, a couple of days later.

"When I went through the train station I happened to catch the eye of the Station Master and I saw on his face a deep scowl," she said and laughed. It seemed to me that finally, in hindsight she could find the circumstance around my train trip amusing.

We spent most of the day talking and looking over travel brochures. That night we went to a dinner show, which she had very much wanted to see. Anna and I got dressed up, me as best I could, since I had not thought to bring any nice clothes, and she in a nice outfit she brought with her from Melbourne.

It was considered a dinner show, but the dinner was served before the show. The menu listed steak. That was about all it listed -- a large steak, T-bone, and a small baked potato. Anna did not want a steak because she was vegetarian. The help was not very cooperative, but finally did serve her a very plain plate of steamed vegetables. Anna commented afterwards that non-vegetarians often think that a vegetarian eats only vegetables, and raw ones at that. My steak was memorable, weighing about a pound.

The show was good. I had a hard time following along, because I did not know the story beforehand. It was about the history of the sheep trade in Australia. There was one song in particular that Anna explained had been changed because of the controversy over a phrase used in the song which the Aborigines found objectionable in later generations. The original song referred to the Aborigines as “Abos.” This was a derogatory term, akin to the American term "Nigger." I forget what she said the politically correct word was that replaced it.

There was a big movement in Australia, by the Aborigines, to reclaim the land. It seems that Aborigines asserted that the white government of Australia had stolen the land away from them. After much debate and in-fighting the Australian government came to the conclusion that the world was looking at them as an oppressive government. They did not want to be viewed like Americans with regard to Native Americans, or like the English treatment of South Africans. Many of the "white” people of Australia, who considered themselves to be the rightful heirs of Australia, were against the government giving back the land to the Aborigines, especially without restrictions.

The next day Anna and I took the Sydney harbor ferry across to Bondi Beach. The view of the harbor was magnificent. The sky was slightly overcast and there was a cold breeze blowing from the East across the harbor littered with sailboats moving fast in the strong wind. Anna pointed out the world-famous Sydney harbor bridge and the area in which her brother lived on the other side of Bondi Beach.

The dock on the ocean side of the harbor ties up on the windward side of Bondi Beach, which sticks out like a finger between the harbor and the ocean. Bondi Beach, is, a small strip of near-white sand. What I remember best was that it was about one hundred meters across and about three-forths of a kilometer long. In reality, it is actually much longer. Maybe the reason I remembered it much smaller is because we stayed on the boardwalk and did not venture into the sand. At Bondi Beach, they enjoy the French Rivera version of sun bathing, topless. This style seemed a big draw to a crowd of tourists and onlookers, mostly men.

From Bondi Beach, we walked down to the Manly Ocean world Aquarium. At the time it was touted to be one of the world's first aquarium's to have a "walkway through aquarium." This was a moving sidewalk that traveled through an enclosed glass tunnel and actually went through the aquarium. It was amazing to actually see a shark or a Monterey swim above you.

During the return ferry excursion, I insisted on riding on the outside deck so I could readily see the harbor, and all its many wonders. Anna did not really like this idea because the wind whipped across the deck and was very cold. Riding on the outside gave us a good view of the the Sydney Harbor Bridge (also known as 'The Coat Hanger' Anna said) and on the way back, the Sydney Opera House.

The Sydney opera house is breathtaking to behold. It is considered by some people an unofficial wonder of the world, Anna told me. I wondered if she might have been saying that out of Australian egocentric patriotism. Even so, I was very fascinated by the opera house and we decided to go to there.

The opera house sat at the end of a peninsula with water surrounding it on three sides. The peninsula extends out from circular quay into Sydney harbor. Even from the ferry terminal, the opera house was spectacular. It was still a good two kilometers away, but Anna and I decided to traverse the distance, anyway. The peninsula was surfaced with polished brick, quite beautiful in itself.

The trek in the hot sun was longer than I had figured. The opera house was larger than I originally imagined, and the walk was actually more like two miles, roughly three-and-one-quarter kilometers. By the time we had arrived at the opera house we were both hot and quite thirsty. There was a concession stand with a big, bold sign proclaiming, "Dogs and 'Ade" (hot dogs and lemonade), so we both stopped and had a super size lemonade.

"This is the best lemonade I've ever had," I loudly proclaimed. The woman who ran the concession beamed with pride, looking around to see if anybody else had heard the proclamation. Anna just looked at me dubiously.

"That lemonade was so g in ood, I think I will have another. Would you like another, Anna?" I asked, although I really didn't think I needed to ask. We both ordered another super size.

"You didn't really mean that, that it was the best lemonade you've ever had, did you?" Anna asked, when we got outside of hearing distance of the woman running the stand.

"No . . . I guess . . . not really," I said in a mock-peevish grin. "It's that when you are hot and thirsty, every cup of lemonade is the best lemonade you have ever had." She laughed and agreed with me.

We made our way to the box office and asked if there was a possibility of venturing inside to look around. The woman in the box office said that they have regular scheduled guided tours, but the tour would not accommodate a wheelchair. The tour follows up and down many flights of stairs into many different auditoriums. I was disappointed and began shaking my head thinking, that I had come all this way and I couldn't see the inside. Besides, I wondered, how do people in wheelchairs get in, even to see a performance. The woman seeing the consternation on my face said to wait a minute and stepped into a room marked "Manager." She returned and said that she personally would take us on a tour of the facility using the backstage elevators.

This tour was exceptional. Riding up and down on the backstage elevators, we went amongst the sets and props that were raised into place from below the stage on several enormous, open-sided, elevators. As we rose onto the stage, from the floor below, we looked out across the auditorium at the regular tour taking place. The woman who was giving us the tour explained that this tour was normally the seventy-five-dollar tour and was given only on Sundays. Because my wheelchair did not accommodate the stairs, and because I had come all the way from America and wanted to see the opera house, they made a special exception and gave us the backstage tour, the Sunday tour, on Saturday, for only ten dollars.

We turned and exited the stage through a doorway, and down a hallway of polished hardwood that lead into another auditorium. Much of the interior was hardwood and plush velvet. The curtains, which hung above the stages, were elegant and finely woven. As we continued the tour, our hostess went on to explain that there were six different auditoriums. She said that the designer of the opera house came up with the design while he was eating an orange one day. As he peeled it, he noticed how the pieces of the peel stood together by sheer pressure. Oranges, he thought, naturally stay clean if it rains. He proceeded to build the sides of the opera house with a natural curve, covering these with tiles that had the texture of an orange, but were white. He butted the two enormous structures of the many roofs together with glue. Of course, it wasn't contact cement, but special steel adhesive. He didn't need to bolt the two roofs together. The entire structure was well-built.

When we left the opera house, the sun was low on the horizon and just about to set. The sunset was awe-inspiring. Walking back across the peninsula, we could not help but notice that the wind had picked up and was pushing us along the walkway. I opened my coat and the wind pushed me along. The walk back was quite brief through the Sydney harbor mall, and we caught a taxi back to the youth hostel.

When we walked into the youth hostel, we checked the bulletin board for any last-minute announcements and saw a flyer for a "Pub Crawl." I asked Anna what a Pub Crawl was and she explained that it was a barhopping ritual, so named because by the end of the evening the participants are usually crawling from one pub to the next. This sounded fun, so we inquired about attending, but the other participants did not want to make the effort to accommodate my wheelchair, so Anna and I didn't go. We were probably better off.

We walked from the hostel a few blocks through a seedy looking neighborhood that Anna explained was ripe with drugs, prostitution and homeless people. We stepped into a small restaurant that had only a few patrons. Of the few people that were there, two looked especially grungy and were probably local residents. We had a quiet and unmemorable meal and walked back to the hostel. Before turning in, Anna phoned her brother, who lived in an area near Manly, just north of Bondi Beach.

That night, after Anna phoned her brother, I decided to call my parents and surprise them. The conversation lasted all of about two minutes. I didn't know the workings of the phones there in Australia, and with Anna's help I dialed the number. It was a little bit after 9 p.m. and I figured that they would still be up.

"Hello . . ." a groggy voice hesitantly said. I recognized it as my mother's.

"Hi, it's Thom, I'm calling from Australia," I said, excitedly, thinking it would be gladly accepted that I had called.

"Oh, hi . . . " I didn't hear my mother saying to my father in the background, "George, grab the other phone, it's Thom calling from Australia," since that's what she always did when someone called that they both wanted to talk to.

"I'm having a great time," I cheerfully said, trying to hide my disappointment in her nonchalant response to hearing my voice. "I am in Sydney now and just saw the opera house."

"Oh, that's nice, Honey," came her hesitant reply. I was nonplussed.

"What time is it, there," I asked, suddenly realizing what the difficultly might be.

"It's just a little after three in the morning," she answered. "Your father and brother are asleep."

I had completely forgotten the time change. Because the eastern seaboard of Australia is on daylight savings time, that would make Los Angeles six hours ahead of Australian time, and one day behind as well. The math of the time difference flashed through my head and I thought to myself, "Duh . . . . Come on, Thom, think about what you're doing. No wonder they aren't interested in hearing from you, it's the middle of the night." It was one of those times when I foolishly acted before I took the time to think.

"Sorry about that, I really hadn't thought about the time difference. But tell everybody hello for me and tell them I'm having a great time. Bye." And that was that. I felt as though nobody cared one way or the other if I was there or not. I knew this wasn't true and that it was a matter of the timing of the call, but it still bugged me.

The next evening Anna's brother, Peter, picked us up from the youth hostel and we went to dinner.

Afterwards they suggested we do King's Cross. They briefly explained that King's Cross was considered the "Hollywood Boulevard" of Sydney. I agreed that we go there, and they corrected me and said, "One, does not GO to King's Cross, one, DOES King's Cross."

Hollywood Boulevard, located in Hollywood, California, is quite something to see and I really expected a treat. Anna's brother drove through King's Cross, down the main drag. It was very short, and before I could see anything, we had been there and done that, we had passed through King's Cross. I thought maybe they were referring to another area on the street. I thought maybe I had blinked and missed something. I asked if we could park and look around. We circled around and Anna's brother found a parking place.

The curb where we parked was cobblestone and uneven. I was having difficulty setting up my chair. It was sitting in a rather precarious position. In the process of transferring to my wheelchair from the car, I misjudged the distance and I pushed too hard. I went over my chair landing head first on the cobblestone sidewalk. The last thing I remember was hearing the loud ring of a church bell.

The next thing I remember was a pale yellow wall and some type of equipment, I could not make it out. I had this vague sense that I was in a hospital. My head was pounding. I was groggy and could not stay awake. I was fading in and out of unconsciousness. I vaguely remember a doctor asking if I had insurance. I must have said no, because he went away and came back laughing and said that the hospital visit would be on them, meaning the Australian government, complements of their socialized medicine. I asked him what he meant, and he laughed even harder, then looked at me seriously and told me that I was in the hospital for a mild concussion and I needed to get stitches in my head. I looked at him perplexed, then faded back off into unconsciousness.

When I woke again, Anna was sitting beside the bed clutching my hand. She looked worried and frightened. She had laid her head down on the bed next to me trying to stay awake. She looked tired and under a lot of strain. I managed to raise my head enough to see into her eyes and said not to worry. I asked her where I was. She smiled gently, then chuckled lightly and said that I was in the hospital. She asked me if I remembered what happened and I told her that I didn't.

I asked her where the church was. She looked at me nonplussed, as if I had said something completely out of context. The expression on her face caused me to laugh, sending a jolt of pain through my head. I had said something funny, but didn't know what it was that I had said.. I explained to her that I had heard a church bell ring. She turned to someone outside my line of vision with an amused twinkle in her eye and I heard a man's laughter from behind me, which I recognized as Anna's brother. She explained to me that the bell I had heard was most likely the one ringing when my head hit the pavement.

After my head was stitched up and I was released, Anna began calling taxi companies, from a phone book she had found in the lobby. We needed to get a ride back to the youth hostel. While she was calling, someone in the hospital mentioned that, there was a taxi service available that would accommodate my wheelchair. Fortunately, when she called there was a taxi available. For the first time on the whole trip, I was able to ride in a taxi that my wheelchair fit without the need to transfer and have the chair folded and stowed in the trunk. We rode back to the youth hostel in style.

"What ?" I asked when I caught Anna watching me out of the corner of my eye, in my turban-looking head bandage.

"You," she said when I turned to face her. She began giggling, then chuckling and finally breaking down into sheer laughter. "You look ridiculous, like a turbaned king."

"Well, I am happy to be of assistance," I responded sarcastically.

"There was something else. When you were unconsciousness, you kept waking up, looking up, and asking me, 'Anna, what the hell am I doing in Australia?' then would fade back off to sleep," she said, hardly being able to contain her laughter.

It was around 5:30 a.m. by the time we got back to the youth hostel. We left a note explaining the situation and requesting that the 9:00 a.m. check-out time be extended to 11 or 12. Neither of us had gotten much sleep during the night. The sleep I had gotten in the hospital, was not really sleep, but was actually unconsciousness.

6

Melbourne Revisited - Where the Skies Are Never Over Los Angeles

The following day, it was noon by the time we had breakfast and headed toward the train station to make the trip back to Melbourne. Because we had plenty of time before our departure, Anna and I, decided to stop in a pub for a beer along the way.

As we walked into the pub there were several local Australians, or what I assumed were locals, from their comfortable air and dress. They were playing pool on a pool table that I had not seen the likes of before. It was made of rough eucalyptus branches, complete with peeling bark, and cut in such a way that the slate table surface, lined with green felt, fit snugly down into the frame. It must have been a true and accurate table because several of the men were evidently in a heated contest and concentrating and giving each other a hard time.

"I don't ever think I have seen such a table. The uniqueness of the table must draw in the customers just to have a chance to play on it," I commented to one of the fellows, breaking his concentration. He turned to me and smiled.

"G'day, mate. I'm glad you like it. I made it for this watering hole a few years back," he said.

I looked around at the furnishings of the pub and saw that most of the tables, chairs, and flooring were made of light-colored wood. I was struck, also, by the fact there was plenty of light in that establishment, unlike the bars here in America, which have a dark stain on the wood and such dark lighting. There were plenty of windows, and most were either beveled or etched with local flora and fauna. I was still looking around when the same fellow noticed my interest, and eyed me with speculation, as if trying to weigh my curiousness as either admiration or something that shouldn't be taken seriously from a man in a wheelchair.

"Where do you hale from? I've not seen you in here before," he said.

"I'm traveling here from America. I live in Venice, California, which is part of Los Angeles," I answered.

"Yeah? I kind of figured, from your accent and get-up that you were a Yank!"

"Yank," Anna leaned over, whispering in my ear, "is Aussie slang for an American."

"What you think of Australia?" he asked.

"Australia is great! So much open space, and so few people. Where I come from we have more people living in Los Angeles than in all of Australia. The weather is great. The people are great and so friendly too." I blurted out, feeling the effects of the beer that I had ordered. I went on to tell him about some of my experiences so far, as well as my impressions of Australia since I had arrived.

"Let me buy you a beer! What are you drinking?"

When I told him, he called over to the waitress and told her to bring me a Piss beer, it was on him. I thanked him and he turned back to his game.

Anna turned to me and said that during the first few days that I was in Sydney, she had been contacted by the hospital, where she had applied, in Melbourne. She had been invited to an interview and was accepted for a position as a Play Therapist. After returning to Melbourne, Anna started her new job while I stayed at the house.

It was during one of these days I dragged the beanbag chair outside into the backyard and climbed into it. I sat lazily starring at the sky, watching the fluffy white clouds drifting across a blue sky. The blue was so vivid and deep it seemed to swallow me up along with my thoughts.

I began drifting back and thinking about some of things I had accomplished and the adventures I had had. Like the defining moment, when I realized that fate truly was in my hands and the circumstances in my life are what I make them to be: It was on a trip I took to Arizona, on a three-wheeled custom motorcycle I had built.

Pushing the engine hard I rode on a long and isolated highway, between Yuma and Hila Bend, a one-hundred-mile-or-so stretch with no fuel or refreshment stops that I could see. I had just passed through a cloud of insects, many of which were bees that stung my face and flew up the sleeves of my coat. I was beating off the bees and I guess the venom from their stings put me into a sort of trance, because the next thing I knew I was mesmerized by the passing asphalt and feeling as though it was melting to swallow up me and my bike.

A thought pushed to the forefront of my mind in a question, "What if I crashed, not wearing a helmet? Would my head smash into the pavement, grinding and pulverizing, becoming one with the asphalt?"

The answer to the question came to my mind in such a nonchalant deadpan way that it surprised even me, "You'd most likely die! Your head would hit the ground and the bike would make mincemeat out of your body as it ran over you. You would wind up in a ditch. That would be that, life over. That's all she wrote."

I don't really know why that thought was comforting. All I know is that I felt it to be comforting. Maybe it's because it became a defining moment, a moment when I knew fate was in my hands, not someone else's.

On the same trip, but a completely different town, after riding for several hours and feeling rather thirsty, I stopped in an establishment that looked like it would have something to drink. The place turned out to be a bar. I dismounted the bike in the parking lot and a patron of the bar, who had been standing in the doorway, commented to me as I passed .

"You have 'cuhunas' the size of watermelons. I would never have the guts to ride that thing," pointing toward the bike. "I can see from your plates that you are from California. You do have more guts than I do," he said. I thought to myself, “I don't know what the big deal is, I'm just living my life.” Yet at the same time, I felt an overwhelming sense of pride in myself.

Then the time when I got pulled over for speeding came to mind. Doing a hundred down the other side of the Grapevine--a narrow, steep, winding pass descending into the Central Valley of California--passing cars and big semi's, between and on the right and left shoulders of the highway. I could see a highway patrolman following me, zigzagging back and forth in my mirror. I figured why should I slow down now, I am already caught speeding. Along about five miles later I heard in the wind-swept air a static-filled, garbled voice.

"Slow down there on the right." I was barely able to make out the words.

I slowed down, to seventy. Two or three exits later as I was getting off the freeway at the exit to the road heading for Kern river, where I planned to spend a relaxing weekend camping out and fishing, I noticed red lights flashing in my mirror. I pulled over.

The patrolman walked up to my motorcycle and said, "I told you pull over back there."

"I thought you said to 'slow down over there,'" I said, "and I did slow down . . . ," I swallowed the lump in my throat and said, barely above a whisper, " . . . to seventy."

He just grinned and gently shook his head, as if to say, 'Yeah, right', and said, "Well, let's see your license and registration."

"Why?" I asked with a dead-pan face.

"Because," he said with a broad smile, which seemed almost an amused smirk, then he leaned against the handlebars and continued, "you were doing 100 mph back there." He started walking around the bike shaking his head. He stopped behind the bike and looked again at the wheelchair and asked, "Have you ever been pulled over for speeding?"

"Yeah, once," I said, scratching my head, "in Arizona, I think."

"In Arizona?" he exclaimed, "you drove this," gesturing towards the bike, "to Arizona?" Then he said, in what sounded like a reluctant tone, "Well I'm going to have to write you a ticket for speeding," pausing, and then continuing, "but I will only write you up for seventy miles per hour." I knew he could have confiscated the keys and arrested me right there, so a ticket for doing seventy I felt was a willing compromise.

I smiled while thinking about the bike (trike actually, but to me it was my bike) and all the good experiences during my days living the biker lifestyle. This got me thinking along the lines of what had been happening at the time I built the trike.

At the time I built the trike, I owned and operated a small print shop, Thom's Print Shop. A small hole-in- the-wall store that I had put together after I had been laid-off while working as a printing pressman, running a Heidelberg "Windmill" Platen Printing Press, for a small mom-and-pop print shop that I got a job at just out of high school. I had no thoughts to go to college or furthering my education in any way. Running a printing press is what I had planned to do for the rest of my life. In my solitary world of running this press, I had no thoughts of what might be going on in the actual world or the economy. Business slowed down to a near standstill, and I got laid off, with the promise that as soon as work picked back up I would be hired back.

Well, in my narrow and catastrophic thinking, I said to myself, "People are not going to hire you with your clutzy disability, so instead of putting yourself through all that humiliation you might as well make yourself a job and buy into or actually buy a working print shop that you can run yourself." Being naïve and full of myself, I believed I could do it. I had no idea what running a business took.

The business, Thom's Print Shop, lasted for less than a year, and during that year I started to use a wheelchair just before Christmas, on my twentieth birthday. Merry Christmas, Thom. Troubled and in turmoil, I began to think about my future.

A couple of years later I went back to school in printing management. I thought that even though I could no longer run a printing press, I could manage a printing establishment. When I finished the trade school I left, not wanting to go through a graduation, with a certificate in Printing Management, I landed a job as a Printing Estimator for a midsize struggling print shop and later, through a half-baked proposal, I moved up into a sales position for the same company. Within a year or so, again unemployed and not knowing about my future, I decided to go back to school. This time it was in an entirely different direction. One that was closer to my heart and my philosophical way of thinking, psychology. I reasoned and justified this way of thinking with the idea that "the disease might take my body, but, dammit all, I will not let it take my mind."

The school I chose to complete my studies in psychology was Sierra University: UWW, the UWW standing for its former name, University Without Walls. A free-thinking educational establishment that based its principles on the philosophical paradigm, badly paraphrased here, "We already contain the knowledge of whatever we are learning, we just need the right experience to bring it forward in our minds." The school believed that one's personal experiences and previous studies were life skills and were in themselves credits toward ones future and could be counted as credits towards a degree.

This philosophy of education fit snugly into my principles of life being its own education and how I needed to take credit for my own learning from my life. I sped through my studies, much of which was home study and research, With the life credits, I had almost enough credits for my Bachelor's degree, and in another two years I received my Master's degree in Psychology, with an emphasis in Marriage, Family and Child Counseling, a six-year endeavor in a regular university. I completed my studies in less than three years.

It was through this change in focus of my life's work that I landed the job as peer counselor at WCIL and subsequently, because of lack of funding, was again out of work and contemplating my future. This is when I decided to pursue the long-lost dream of going to Australia.

As I lay there contemplating my trip in Australia and watching the fluffy white clouds drifting across the amazingly blue sky, it suddenly occurred to me that "This sky is not over Los Angeles." Now, I knew logically that the world was spinning and that at any particular second no part of the earth is ever under the same sky for any duration longer than a sheer fragment of a moment, and although the idea that this sky was not over, and I was not under, the same skies of Los Angeles was not exactly true. The idea was so powerful, it made the whole trip to Australia seem beyond description. The entire experience took on an ethereal feeling. This was the reason I had come to Australia. It was a defining moment. I felt free. I didn't have that old familiar feeling that people treated me differently, or made judgments about me. I was just another person. What people thought didn't really matter. Nothing mattered more than this moment. I was content. I WAS IN AUSTRALIA.

On another day, I contacted Dave, who I had met during the layover in New Zealand. He came down and picked me up, and we drove back to his place. His house was a small one-bedroom place in the mountains about twenty-five kilometers east of Melbourne. It was surrounded by trees in a very rural area spread over several hills. The house was located on a road that wound through the hills, and once in awhile I could see a few other houses hidden amongst the trees and underbrush as we drove along the road. There were many farms in the surrounding area. However, this area did not look suitable for farming. On the drive up he explained that he had applied his trade, as a pottery maker, and found a niche for himself. He had managed to establish himself in a lucrative business. He said he originally had about forty acres, but wound up selling all but five acres. A few years back his house had burnt to the ground and he had rebuilt the one he and his wife now lived, using the money from the sale of land.

When we arrived, he took me on a brief tour of the house and introduced me to his wife. After I got settled in, we went out onto his back porch overlooking a wild grassy area surrounded by trees about thirty feet back. I commented to him that my normally keen sense of direction had suddenly become a problem. I explained. “I usually have an innate sense of direction, based on the compass.” I went on to explain. “Many times when Anna and I would go places I would try to get a sense of where we were headed, so I could return home on my own if I wanted to. But, for some reason, I kept getting my directions all wrong. I always figured the directions ninety degrees off the compass. For example, if we were traveling down one street and we’d turn to go down another, based on my knowledge of the sun and shadows, I would tell Anna if we were heading North or East or West, depending on which way we had started out. Some eighty percent of the time, I was wrong.:

“That’s because we’re on the other side of the world. The sun is casting from a different direction,” he said quietly, chuckling.

I thought about this, contemplating what he had said, and it occurred to me where the difficulty arose.

"Ah! I think I see,” I said. “Our inner sense of direction is based, not on the sun, which is often believed, but on the shadows, and the directions that are being cast. Subconsciously, we note where the sun is in its zenith and how the shadows are being cast. This process takes place totally without our conscious awareness."

"Yes. That's right," he replied. "When we are on the other side of the world, meaning above or below the equator, the sun is casting the shadows in a slightly different direction. If we haven't taken into account the fact that we are now on the earth far enough above or below the equator, our internal compass becomes skewed slightly. Slightly, is a keyword here. The streets in a city do not follow true compass directions, so the slight variance in the cast of the shadows can throw a person's inner sense of directions ninety degrees off."

Once the problem with my inner sense of direction had been defined, the solution almost explained itself. My inner sense of direction was resolved. Knowing the directions ceased to be a difficulty for me the remainder of the trip.

While we were sitting on his porch, a wild kangaroo came bounding by, hopping in a comical way and disappearing in the cluster of trees at the end of his yard. The kangaroo was ruddy brown in color. It stood still at one point, and when standing still it stood looking at us with a magnificent grace and pride, as if to say, "THIS IS MY YARD, WHAT ARE YOU PEOPLE DOING HERE?"

"This kangaroo often shows itself in the yard and does this same thing every time it comes through," he said with evident pride. He could see the amazement in my eyes.

He went on to explain that these brushes with raw nature often happen in rural areas. It brought pictures to my mind of how closely I imagined Australia was to being wild. I did not know what to expect Australia to be like, but try as I did, I still unconsciously formed a picture of Australia as being a backward country in much the same way I unconsciously formed a picture of other countries, such as Mexico or El Salvador, being primitive and backwards with little or no running water and having dirt roads. As illogical as this was, I was grateful to have my former illusions broken.

The sun set, but it was still quite pleasant. Dave's wife served dinner outside, which was steak and potatoes. After dinner, though it was still warm, we went back into the house, where he dug a ten or twelve-inch TV out of his closet and we watched an old American classic, "Blade Runner." After the movie, we turned in.

The next day we drove from his place about twenty miles to the Koala reserve. On the way there, we made a side trip and stopped at a small medical clinic to have the stitches in my head removed. Back on track, we drove the remaining few miles to the reserve. It was a forty or fifty-acre parcel of land filled with eucalyptus trees. We walked down the main road and saw several koalas that appeared to be lounging in the trees. He then drove me back to where Anna was staying.

The next morning I woke up to a very unpleasant situation. I jerked awake and jumped into my chair and raced down the hall to the lu. My leg bag (urine collection bag) was full, beyond full, it was overflowing. The back flow valve, a small rubber valve that keeps the urine from flowing out of the bag and back up the collection tube, was missing. The urine was back-flowing into my pants, down my legs and onto the nice plush pile rug. I guess in my panic and haste I had made a commotion and had woken up Anna. Because in my mad rush to get to the lu, I saw, out of the corner of my eye, Anna running behind me with a towel, mopping up the floor. I was very embarrassed. Where she got her quick thinking to grab that towel, I still can't say.

I realized what had happened. I had taken a bath while I was at Dave's house. In his efforts to be helpful, he picked up my leg bag to empty it, and inadvertently flushed the back-flow valve down the toilet.

That morning, after Anna had gone to her new job, I looked in the phone book and found what would now be called an Independent Living Center within walking distance. I consulted Anna's street map, and not judging the distance very well, I set out to see if the ILC might have a back-flow valve, or something that I could use. I was still not totally used to the direction of the traffic flow. Cars and even passing pedestrians would suddenly appear before me, and several times, I nearly became someone's hood ornament. I proceeded down numerous suburban streets and entered a divided thoroughfare lined with store fronts. The parking was parallel in front of each store and there was no sidewalk. I was forced to go around the back of each car, placing me directly in the line of traffic.

I finally made it to the ILC. I was slightly disappointed, because it was not that notable. They did, although, have the part that I needed. It had been a difficult, and at times perilous, two miles to get to the ILC, and I had another difficult and perilous two miles to get back. I made it back to the house and had to wait for Anna to get home, because, in my haste to leave, I had locked up but I had forgotten to get the key to the house. I didn't mind waiting though -- I was in Australia.

On one of the last days I was in Melbourne, I woke up late. Anna and I had stayed up late to watch a movie the night before. She had already left for work. She did not need as much sleep as I did. When I woke up, I was ravenous. Anna and I had not been to the store for a few days. There was nothing in the house to eat except a jar of "Vegemite." Vegemite is one of several yeast extract spreads sold in Australia. It is made from leftover brewers' yeast extract (a by-product of beer manufacture) and various vegetable and spice additives. It is very dark reddish-brown, almost black, in color, and one of the richest sources known of Vitamin B. It's thick like peanut butter, it's very salty, and it tastes like - well let's just say that it is an acquired taste! A Vegemite sandwich to an Australian kid is the equivalent of a peanut butter and jelly sandwich to an American kid.

I had read about Vegemite and the idea of having a Vegemite sandwich intrigued me. The idea had been the craze in America since that well-liked song by the Australian group, Men at Work. In their song, "Down Under," the words of the chorus go:

Do you come from a land down under?
Where women glow and men plunder?
Can't you hear, can't you hear the thunder?
You better run, you better take cover.

Buying bread from a man in Brussels
He was six foot four and full of muscles
I said, "Do you speak-a my language?"
He just smiled and gave me a vegemite sandwich...

A few days earlier, I had wanted to try a Vegemite sandwich, so Anna made one for me. A nice one, just like they are recommended, bread-and-butter with a thin layer of Vegemite over the butter. Maybe she had made it too thick, I mean the layer of Vegemite, because it was not what I had expected. I was thinking along the lines of a peanut butter sandwich. What I got was quite different. It was a chewy, salty, sharp, bitter, yeasty flavor that I did not wholly like. I figured it must be as I read, an acquired taste.

Anyway, as I was saying, there was nothing in the house to eat. I could not readily go to a store. I had no idea where one would be. I thought about going to the pizza parlor, but I did not know if they would be open. Also, I was feeling pretty lazy. I could have left the house and looked for someplace to fill my stomach. But, being very hungry and not thinking right, I found a bottle of bourbon whiskey in one of the cupboards. I began thinking, "Bourbon, it is made from sour mash, and mash is just chopped up vegetables, this will fill my stomach." I probably don't have to tell you the rest of the story, but, not having had anything to eat, and after having two or three glasses, and wondering why I was not getting full, I was pretty drunk.

It was soon apparent that I had no idea what time it was. Anna's sister, Mary, who had accompanied Anna and I on our excursion to Philip Island, showed up and said that Anna had called her from work and asked her to pick me up. Anna wanted to go to a local fair, a semi-permanent establishment, like an amusement park. Mary came to get me and found me in my befuddled state, three-sheets-to-the-wind, and didn't know what we should do. She helped me up the ramp to where I changed and got ready to go. Being pretty drunk, I attempted to roll down the ramp by myself. I rolled fast to the bottom of the ramp, until I got to the sharp angle where the ramp met the floor. The front wheels of my chair did not roll smoothly onto the floor of the kitchen, but dug in and I plunged, head first, onto the floor. Anna's sister was pretty disgusted by then. And I couldn't blame her. She just sat down and left me to climb back into my chair. We drove to the fair, but I have only one recollection of the evening. Sitting in the dark, huddling myself to keep warm, Anna and Mary went inside a coffee establishment. They were too embarrassed to take me inside. I do not remember getting home.

7

Adelaide - Burning Indelible Traces

I had been in Melbourne for five or six days, when I realized I had only about ten or so days left before I had to use my return ticket back to the States. I was anxious to get as much traveling in before I had to leave as I could. I wanted to see much more of Australia. There was a town located near the center of Australia, called Alice Springs. The idea of being in the center of all Australia tantalized me, and I wanted to go there. Because the airlines were still on strike nationwide, my best option was taking a train called "the Overland" from Melbourne to Adelaide, then transferring to another train called "The Ghan" for the remaining leg to Alice Springs.

Anna had told me that Adelaide was known as the "church city" of Australia, because it had more churches per capita than any other city in Australia. I never found out if this was true, but I found it an interesting thought.

The train ride was not a very memorable segment of my journey, except that it was fairly flat and all I could see out my window were trees, and a good portion of the leg was at night. The train stopped several times to pick up and disembark different passengers in small towns along the way to Adelaide.

When I reached my destination, the station gave me this feeling that I was stepping through time into the Old West. My surroundings could have doubled for a scene out of an old western movie. The station was all of about twenty feet long, the walls had wood shingles and the landing was of what appeared to be of six- or eight-inch wide rough-hewn boards, worn and scuffed to a polish. They extended out past the building towards the rear of the train. The ticket office faced the landing under a large overhang that was part of the roof of the building.

I walked down the landing, feeling as though I was rolling over a washboard. My head was bouncing up and down so much that I nearly rolled off the edge because I couldn't see. I found where my luggage had been unloaded and began to get oriented to my surroundings. I loaded my backpack on the back of the wheelchair and got the other bag situated underneath. I asked the man who was handling the luggage where we were in relation to the actual city of Adelaide. He scratched his head, reaching under his hat, looked thoughtfully for a moment , and said, in that dry nasal twang that Australians have, that the town was about six kilometers, down the narrow two-lane road, over a one-way bridge and through the main park. I thanked him and said that I would walk into town.

"You can't do that, it's too far," said a woman, overhearing the conversation with concern and mixed amazement. "Let me flag down a taxi for you."

"No thank you," I politely refused.

"No, no, it's really too far. The taxi stand is right outside. I will flag one down for you."

"I'd rather walk, or push actually," I said again. "It's a nice day and I'd rather walk, having been cooped up in the train all night." I did not know that there was a prediction for rain in the forecast for that day. The last I saw of that woman, she was walking away shaking her head.

The walk, or push, was not simple. Traversing the narrow road was tricky. There was quite a bit of traffic, and being unused to the direction of the traffic flow I found myself often slipping off the pavement. One time when my back wheels slipped off the pavement, they embedded themselves in mud in a piece of ground recently soaked by rain. It was the first time I noticed that it had recently rained and the area might be due for some more. I took the bags and backpack off the chair and reached out and gently set them on a piece of ground that looked solid enough. I climbed out of the chair and extricated the back wheels from the mud. When I picked up the backpack I saw that the piece of ground that I set the stuff on was only surface dry, and the bottom of my backpack was wet. I climbed back into the chair, rearranged the stuff and continued on my way.

When I got to the bridge that the station hand had mentioned, I had to wait quite a while for the traffic to clear enough for a safe crossing. Traversing across the up side of the bridge, my chair turned over backwards spilling me and my bags all over the road. I gathered up my stuff, climbed back into the chair, rearranged the bags, and continued on my way. Fortunately, the bridge was not as long as if it appeared from the side I started, and I encountered no cars.

As I continued to push my way along, I came to a park area that was quite large. I would estimate about a mile wide. I was about a mile out of town, and it began to get cloudy and started to rain. Not hard, but hard enough that I needed to look for cover. I spied some trees in the park up ahead. I pushed a little faster and when I got to the tree, I dug in my pocket for the map of Adelaide that I had gotten in the train station. I could see that the youth hostel I was looking for was several more blocks into town, once I actually reached the outskirts. I worked my way along, going from tree to tree, as the rain would lighten. I was still a few blocks from town.

"Do you need a ride?" I heard, but didn't know exactly where the voice came from. "Over here," and I looked toward the road and saw a woman had stopped who was traveling in the opposite direction I was going. She had rolled down her window and was calling from there.

"No thanks, "I called out. “It's only a few more blocks to town, and besides, you're going the other direction."

"Are you sure you don't need a ride ?" she called out. I turned in her direction and she had turned around, stopped and rolled down her other window. I quickly glanced at the map again and calculated how far it was and how long it would take to go the remaining way to the youth hostel. Being wet and cold, I decided a ride would be nice.

"Actually, a ride would be great, but I am wet and awful dirty and I have a lot of baggage and my chair won't fit in your car," I answered.

"I can always clean the seats and I can put the bags in the back seat. As for your wheelchair, it folds doesn't it," she said, and continued before I could respond, "I can put it in the trunk. It doesn't have to go in all the way."

I told her where I was going, and she responded by saying she knew just where the hostel was located. I climbed in and she put my bags and my wheelchair into the car. Along the way, we talked. I explained that I was from America, and proceeded to tell her about some of my adventure so far. She introduced herself as Corinne and said that it was no hardship to give me a ride to town.

We were still a few blocks from the youth hostel when we were pulled over by the police. She quickly reached over and made sure that my seat belt was fastened. She said that in Australia there was a law that seat belts must be fastened and that it was a very heavy fine for noncompliance. The policemen was questioning the wheelchair in the trunk and the trunk not being all the way closed. She explained that she was giving a ride to a traveler from America and that she only had to go only a few more blocks and that she was going to drop me off. He let her off with a warning.

When we arrived at the hostel, she helped me with my chair and baggage, and as she was leaving she asked me to have dinner and go to a show with her that evening. We arranged for her to pick me up about 6 p.m. I looked at my watch, and it was almost four o'clock. I had spent most of the day pushing from the train station.

It turned out that the youth hostel was accessible, complete with widened doors and a fully equipped bathroom with a toilet and roll-in shower. I settled in, and by the time I had managed to change and clean up it was nearly 6 o'clock.

She arrived, as promised right at 6, and off we went. It turned out that the dinner she had in mind was with her friends at their home. The dinner was typical of Australian cuisine--meat and potatoes. When we sat down for dinner, they asked me if I would like any coffee and how I liked it. I said yes, and that I would like it black. The host then commented by saying, "Oh, of course! You are from America, I forgot. Of course you would want that 'Yank coffee,'"

The dinner gave me another opportunity to get to know the people and hear more stories about Australia. Afterwards, we all got into our separate cars and went to "the show," which turned out to be at her church. I am not very religious, but it gave me an idea of the religious tenets of this particular group of church goers in Adelaide. It was very vocal and boisterous, with a lot of speaking in tongues, and a call for converters. After the service, there were refreshments and she introduced me to many of her friends. She then invited me to go with her to an art exhibit opening of a friend's paintings in the morning. Afterwards she would take me back to the train station to catch the train for my remaining leg of the trip to Alice Springs.

At 9 o'clock the next morning, I had all my baggage lined up in front of the youth hostel waiting . . . and waiting some more. Just when I was beginning to think that she wasn't coming and I would have to call for a taxi to avoid walking all the way back to the train station, Corinne drove up, explaining she had overslept. By then, I was jones-ing for a cup of coffee and thought about asking her to stop. But then I kept thinking about the fact that she had given me a ride upon my arrival and taken me to dinner and to her church. Now she was taking me to an art exhibit of her friends, then driving me back to the station. I shouldn't ask her now, I thought. As we were pulling away, she reached into the console of her car and pulled out a steaming cup of coffee and handed it to me, stating that she didn't drink coffee, but she noticed last night that I did. That cup of coffee was good, the best coffee I had ever tasted.

The art gallery was about two kilometers out of Adelaide, to the north. The art was indeed good, even though I didn't feel I had a real understanding of the finer points of her work. I actually didn't see much of the exhibit, because I was more interested in the people, the neighborhood, the architecture and her. She was quite pretty, and had an unassuming way about her that I found very attractive.

It was early afternoon when Corinne finally took me back to the train station. She walked with me up to the ticket counter to ask about the train. The man behind the counter said that a Road-Train had struck the train and derailed it just outside of town. The man behind the counter said that the train would be delayed between four to six hours.

A Road-Train is a semi-tractor trailer truck. It's built with a big engine and extra torque on a standard chassis and pulls typically four , but as many as twelve, long trailers. Because the towns in Australia are so far apart, sometimes as much as six hundred to a thousand miles, the Australian truck companies have developed this mode of transporting goods between the towns. When people see a Road-Train coming, which is tell-tale from the cloud of dust following it as it comes barreling down the road, they pull off to the side to let it pass. The sheer weight of this truck could easily derail a train.

"We can go back to my place for a few hours," she said, upon hearing the announcement. She turned toward me and with a glint in her eye, and a wicked smile. I had not known that my attraction toward her was that obvious, and I surely had no idea that the attraction was mutual. We left the station, got into her car and drove to her place. A few hours later she drove me back to the station and walked me in. She leaned over and gave me a long, deep, passionate kiss that burned indelible traces in my memory. She straightened up, turned and left. I quietly waited for the train.

8

Alice Springs - Where "You Can Only Get Channel 7"

I had a four- or five-hour wait for the train, so I took out the literature I had on Alice Springs. It wasn't much, since I enjoyed the idea of not planning ahead too much. Still, I needed to think about what I was going to do when I got there. The train station, I noted while I waited, was built much like the one in Adelaide. I got thinking about this, then butted my hand up against my forehead and thought, "Duh! Of course it looks like the same station, it is the same station."

The train for Alice Springs finally arrived, and it looked as if it had come from another era. It had, in fact, been fashioned after the classic style of the 20s or 30s of the outback of Australia, to give the passengers a feel for that period of time. Actually, it could have been built in the 20 or 30s, and well-maintained, for all I knew. The train was called "The Ghan," and I discovered the reason one has to change trains in Adelaide is because the Ghan runs on a different gauge of track, on a narrower gauge, from the Overland.

I was loaded onto the train first, as is usually the case, and my chair was tucked into a forward closet or baggage area. Because I was in the first row of the compartment, I could only see out of about the last quarter of the side window, which was actually the window for the seat behind me. I was confined to my seat and could not go back to the dining car.

Fortunately my fellow passengers realized this, and offered to get me something from the dining car and bring it to me. I really appreciated this gesture, because I had brought nothing to eat for the trip between Melbourne, all the way to Alice Springs, other than a few of Anna's homemade muffins. At that point, I had only one left.

The train ride to Alice Springs was long and tedious, and the steady clacking of the rails was hypnotic. The twenty-one-hour train ride passed very slowly.

I finally arrived in Alice Springs in the early evening. The sun was just beginning to set and I knew I needed to find a place to stay for the night. I really didn't want to spend it in the train station. After gathering all my belongings together I made my way to the information counter to ask where the nearest youth hostel, or inexpensive motel was located. As I was asking the desk clerk for information, a man standing behind me, intervened and said that he ran a private backpacker hostel at a reasonable rate on the north side of town. He said his van was full, but he would come back for me if I wanted. This was a good break, and I readily agreed. I lined myself up by the curb and waited. And waited. I remember thinking that Australian time must be similar to Jamaican time, "Soon come, time." It was getting on towards nine o'clock and I was beginning to think that maybe he had been handing me a line. I was just about to go back into the train station to ask again about lodging when he pulled up with his van. It resembled a Volkswagen van from the 60s, but was actually a van made in Australia, with dual, inside, rear axles, that looked very similar to a VW. He helped into the front seat, loaded my chair and my bags in the back and we headed for the hostel.

Along the way, we talked on and on about Alice Springs and the surrounding area. He introduced himself as Johan, and then added that most people just call him George. One of the sites he recommended I see was Ayers Rock. He said the Australian government had given it back to the Aborigines, who called it Uluru. He added that most Australians continue to call it Ayers Rock, as he said most of the rest of the world does. I thought this somewhat disrespectful to the Aboriginal culture.

As we pulled into the hostel, he told me a little bit about the set up. The hostel was basically several bungalows, with three to five beds and a separate bathroom and toilet in each. As we were walking towards the bungalow I was to stay in, I asked him whether the shower was equipped with a shower seat, and he asked what that was. I explained that it was just some type of chair that I could use in the shower because I had a hard time getting from the floor of the shower into my chair. He stopped next to a metal chair coated with plastic that was sitting at one on the tables outside, and asked whether it would do. I said yes, and he quickly placed it in the shower for me. He said that after I got settled in to come to the office and join him and his family for dinner and a beer. I accepted. A dinner and beer would be welcome because I was hungry. And I thought this was nice because, after all, I had just met him.

The dinner was the usual Australia-type dinner of steak and potatoes. He asked me about my travels, so far and was quite amazed when I told him that I was basically backpacking across Australia, or as far as I could go in the remaining time I had before I went back to America. He had trouble believing that I had started my trip to Australia with nothing more than a round-trip ticket. He introduced me to his wife and three children; two boys--six and eight--and a girl, about three or four. After dinner, we had a few more beers. It was getting late and I was still worn out from the train ride so I said goodnight and returned to my bungalow.

In the room I was getting settled in for the night, when I came across a little plastic, engraved sign affixed to the television, with the words, "You Can Watch Any Station You Want, But We Only Get Channel 7". I looked at this, trying to figure out what it meant and turned on the television. Low and behold, the only channel I got was Channel 7. I found this quite amusing.

When I woke up the next morning, I was feeling a bit unsteady and sluggish because I had consumed more beer than I should have. I started out of my bungalow, thinking I would attempt to find some place to get some coffee. My neighbors in the next bungalow saw me as I was passing, and invited me in for some eggs and coffee. Their bungalow was identical to the one I was staying in. I was not in a very talkative mood, being hung-over as I was, so I quickly finished, thanked them for the breakfast and left. On the way out the door, I noticed the same little plastic engraved sign on the TV in their bungalow as the one in mine.

Feeling fortified by the coffee and the breakfast I went to the office to find a map of Alice Springs. I had one already, but it was only a stick map and I wanted something more detailed. As I was looking through the maps they had in the office, I mentioned seeing the little sign on the televisions.

"Yes," I said chuckling, "in Alice Springs, you can only get in Channel 7. I tried the television last night before I went to bed and only Channel 7 came in. How did you ever think to put a sign like that on the televisions?"

"You like that, do you? One of the backpacker's mentioned the fact that only Channel 7 came in. I had never really thought about it that much, but I realized that he was right and I thought it would be funny to put a little sign on each television to tell the watchers what they CAN'T watch." He said.

I thought this was very funny, a witty turn of phrase, and said so. There was some literature explaining the different sites to see around town. I looked them over with some interest, but I was much more intrigued with getting to know the town, so I found a map that would enable me to get downtown.

"I hate to tell you the bad news, but you don't walk, and besides it's too far," he said, after I mentioned that I'd walk into town.

"You're right," I said with a smile, catching the irony in my own statement, "I don't walk. I roll. My wheels are like my legs though, rolling is still walking to me. We all walk in our own ways."

He admitted that this was true.

Going into town gave me the opportunity to see how the houses were built. Many of the houses and neighborhoods looked like any other house and neighborhood in the States, except the houses looked as though they were in the English countryside.

I was quite surprised that many of the curbs and sidewalks had been cut for curb cuts. The curb cuts at the corners were quite steep by American standards, but the curbs were cut just the same. This was even before the United States had the ADA and the Australian government did not have anything of the sort, either.

Before I reached the downtown area, I decided to stop in an outdoor mall. It was not much of a mall by American standards, just a few stores and a couple of restaurants, but I was hot and hungry. I had been pushing for three or four miles. One of the restaurants was a steak house, and I recalled something my father had told me about meat in Australia. He claimed it was tough and stringy. Though the meat I had previously had in Australia was not like this, I decided to investigate. I looked at the menu, trying to decide what I wanted, but chided myself, because, after all, I was in a steak house. I ordered a steak that would be equivalent to a T-bone. When the steak came I dug in with salivating delight and found that far from being tough and stringy, it was tender and moist and quite flavorful. I asked the waiter about this, and he said that the meat in Australia, whether it comes from cattle or some other type of animal, comes from free-range animals. In America or Canada the meat comes from ranches where the animals are penned to fatten them up before slaughter.

During the walk back to the hostel, it started to rain. Because it was a pretty warm day, the rain felt good. I was enjoying the coolness and fragrance of eucalyptus mixed with the ozone of the fresh rain. It was wonderful and exotic. A couple of times people stopped in their cars to ask if I wanted a ride. When someone would ask me if I "wanted," rather than "needed," a ride, I always felt that it was because they were seeing ME rather than just seeing my wheelchair. But either way, I turned them down, saying that the rain felt good. About an hour into the journey the rain had not let up, and I was thoroughly soaked. All of a sudden, it stopped raining and to my amazement, by the time I got back to the hostel where I was staying I was completely dry.

On the way to my room, I stopped in the office and saw a sign for a camping excursion to Uluru. I asked George what it meant by "camping tour." He explained it was basically a tour where the participants spend the night camping in the Outback. He added that he had taken the tour himself, and that it was quite fun. It was kind of laid-back and the tour guide didn't rush from place to place. He assured me it was not like a commercial tour, bound by schedules and times. This appealed to me, the idea of sleeping in the open in the Outback. I remembered the book from my teenage years with the little creature, and I wondered what it would be like to actually live in the Outback. I immediately signed up for the tour. It ended up being the only tour I took during the entire adventure.

9

Uluru - Rising to Engulf My Spirit

As it turned out, the hostel was the starting point for the camping tour. Participants came from other locations to the backpacker hostel to board the bus. The tour guide did not think twice about how I was going to ride with the group. He immediately assigned two of the passengers to pick me up. One positioned himself under my knees and the other under my shoulders, and together they carried me on to the bus. Another would fold my wheelchair and stow it on the bus behind us. The other passengers were a group of German students who spoke very little English. They were happy to be of assistance.

Uluru is about four-hundred kilometers (roughly three-hundred miles) southwest of Alice Springs, which meant a long drive to our destination. The journey was a reminder of just how big Australia actually is. At one point on the trip, we turned off the highway onto a side road of grated dirt, where the van kicked up dust and gravel for miles. Just as I began to think that maybe the tour guide was lost, maybe he didn't know the route as well as he should have, we turned into a short road with a settlement of five or six houses surrounding a small courtyard. It was about the size of a small town square, but looked more like someone's backyard. It had chickens running around and rolls of chicken wire that had yet to materialize into a chicken coop. There was a broken white picket fence surrounding what could have been a fountain, but looked more like a well or watering trough. The courtyard was littered with trash, which obviously didn't bother the residents of the settlement. As we made our way from the van into the settlement, I found my way into a small tourist trap store that sold everything from Aboriginal art to camera film. At one end of the store was a small lunch counter that was closed for business in the middle of the afternoon.

I struck up a conversation with one of the local men, and inquired about how far our present location was from the highway. He said with a chuckle, that it was seventy or eighty kilometers., though, he had never measured the distance himself. When we left the settlement, I assumed the driver would turn down the road we had come in on, but instead we headed in the same direction we were traveling before. The road we continued to drive on was nearly as long as the road we had driven on to get there. This put the settlement truly out in the middle of nowhere.

After many more miles of bumpy road, we finally arrived at our first destination. Uluru, could be seen from many miles away as the great monolith rose from the ground and grew larger and larger as we approached. It reminded me of being a kid and going to Disneyland, and becoming more excited as the tallest structure, the Mattahorn, gradually grew more visible. The van pulled up and parked in a spot where Uluru towered before us. My first impression was that it was about three-hundred feet high and about one- quarter mile long. Later I found out that it was actually about a thousand feet high and over a mile long on the facing side, in a bloated triangle shape, and about nine miles in circumference. Uluru is an enormous piece of the earth's crust that ruptured out of the ground when the earth was still forming. It turned on its end and most of its enormous size was under the surface of the earth, similar to an iceberg which has ninety or ninety-five percnetof its mass is under the surface of the water. What is jutting out of the ground is only about eight percent of is estimated mass.

There is a great tradition known as "walking Ayers Rock." People climb to the top with the aid of a safety line attached to poles set about ten or twelve feet apart, giving the climbers a steep, but easier, climb up one side of the rock. While the rest the group opted to climb to the top, I decided I would proceed around the base.

The pushing was not that difficult, because the ground had been firmly packed from thousands of other people who had walked the path. I did not get too far though, because when I got out of hearing range of the bustling sounds of the crowds of people and cars an amazing thing happened. Amazing, is an understatement. Awe-inspiring, is closer. Spiritual, that's it. Uluru seemed to raise up and engulf my spirit. I found myself just sitting there in awe. How, I thought, did this come to be? This enormous monolith in the middle of nowhere. I am not religious, but I would say I could feel a divine presence. I could understand how and why the Aborigine people found Uluru such a powerfully spiritual place. It is part of where God resides and actually is part of their God. Uluru is at the center of Aboriginal beliefs and religion.

The group who had opted to climb the rock had returned and were ready to leave, only to find that I had not returned from my excursion around the base. Two of my fellow travelers came to look for me. I did not get nearly as far as I wanted to go, because of my spiritual experience, but I had gotten near the one end, about one-quarter of the distance. When they found me, I was not ready to leave and they had to plead with me to go. As it was, it took nearly five minutes at a jogging pace to rejoin the rest of the group. My other fellow travelers were very impatient with me and let me know it. I thought it kind of amusing that I had not wanted to leave this place just yet.

From Uluru we drove to the Uluru Resort. It had been built to accommodate the thousands of tourists who came to see Uluru each year. The resort was basically just a few overpriced stores and a very overpriced hotel. We milled about the resort until near sunset, when the tour guide said that we would now get the "sunset view" that had been promised in the brochure. We all climbed back into the bus and drove back to Uluru. We parked about one mile to the West of Uluru in a lookout area that was designed specifically for the purpose of viewing Uluru at sunset. The driver, who had done this several times before, knew to arrive early in order to get the best viewing spot for this amazing sight. The tour operator then pulled out a jug of homemade wine, which he said he made for just this occasion of viewing Uluru at sunset. The wine was fruity and much thicker than most wines, but quite good. He then said that whoever wanted could climb onto the bus and view the sunset from the roof.

I never could have anticipated the sight we saw that evening. The descriptions in the brochures couldn't even hold a candle to the actual experience. As the sun sets, it casts its last beams of light across the desert until it strikes the face of Uluru. Gradually and gently the face of Uluru is transformed from a darkest red, to gradually lighter and brighter shades of red, until it finally begins to actually become a glowing red. Picture a pool of molten lava, a shade darker, and you would be seeing Uluru at sunset. It is a total transfiguration and a sight to behold. I will forever remember this vision.

We stayed at Uluru almost an hour and a half past sunset, before climbing back into the bus without a word between us. We drove to the camp ground where we would be spending the night, and with only the light of a kerosene lantern, we prepared a fish dinner fit for kings. A fire was built and we sat around laughing and joking, much of it in German, so I could understand little, and drank the beer we had all chipped in for when we were at the resort. One by one, we slowly drifted away from the fire, chose our different spaces in the camping area, laid out our sleeping bags and climbed in to go to sleep. It was a bit of a challenge for me because I could not see what I was doing. I need to be able to see to be able to feel. The night was very cold, and I did not get much sleep. In the desert it is hot during the day and freezing at night. Around 5:30 in the morning, the tour guide rousted us up. We were all grumbling and hated him for this because we had just turned in a few hours earlier. But we were off to see Uluru at sunrise. We were the only tourists in the lookout area. The tour guide had a surprise for us when we got there and stepped out of the van. A gathering of people we had not met before met our tour group carrying a freshly cooked breakfast, consisting of bacon and eggs and coffee, which we all welcomed with much enthusiasm. Especially the coffee. This was part of the tour that the tour guide said he doesn't tell anyone about, keeping it a secret, even from the brochure, and asked us to keep it to ourselves, to keep the secret alive. It was with much reluctance that I and my fellow travelers said goodbye to Uluru, climbed back in the bus and rode back to Alice Springs in silence. I was grateful however, because I was able to catch up on much-needed sleep, as were the others.

When we got back to the backpacker hostel I turned on the television to watch the news, which reported that the airline strike was over. The negotiations had been settled during the time I had been on the tour. Given this information, I determined that instead of taking the long trip on the train to Melbourne, I should see about flying back to connect to my flight back to the States. But I thought, well hell, I had already purchased roundtrip thickets on the train and why waste them? I went up to the hostel office to ask George if he would be willing to drive me to the train station in the morning. He agreed, and the next morning as we were driving there, I kept thinking about the long ride back.

"Does Alice Springs have an airport," I turned to him suddenly, having made the last minute decision in my head, and asked.

"Yes," he said, chuckling, "Alice Springs is not that backwards."

"Is it big enough for commercial flights?"

"Yes."

"Well, take me there instead of the train station."

"Why? What do you have in mind?" He asked, turning towards me in surprise.

"I am going to fly back to Melbourne, being that the air strike has been settled," I announced, firmly, making it clear that the discussion was over, and there was no room to argue. But argue he did.

"You don't have a ticket. How do you expect to fly back to Melbourne?"

"I'll get a ticket. You watch. Just take me there," I said. He shook his head, but drove me to the airport.

He dropped me off in front of the airport, saying that he had to do some errands and needed to run, but would come back and get me and take me to the train station. He did not believe that I could get a ticket. I walked into the airport, which was about the size of a small bus station, with much the same feel. When I arrived all of the ticket counters, of which there were two, were still closed. While I waited for them to open I wandered through the gift shop and wanted to buy a hat, but they would not take travelers checks, which was all I had left. I was disappointed, but figured I would probably not wear it anyway. Finally, one of the counters came open and I was the first in line and I promptly said I had a reserved ticket to Melbourne, but had forgotten my ticket back in my motel room. The man behind the counter punched in my name and said that there was no reservation under my name. I said there must be a mistake and he punched in my name again and said no reservation under my name, but he did say that there was one seat that had been reserved with no name. I said, that was my ticket and that the guy on the phone probably could not understand me over the phone so did not put a name on the ticket, but I was sure that was my ticket and paid. I was gambling that the person who the ticket belonged to would not show up and claim it.

I went back to the seating area to wait for the plane when George, from the hostel, walked in. He looked as if he expected to take me back to the train station and was quite surprised when I showed him the ticket. He took it from me and looked it over skeptically, but returned it to me, shaking his head. He shook my hand and said "See Ya,' Mate, good luck."

10

Return to Melbourne and the Flight Out

When it came time to board the plane, the other passengers and I were led out onto the airfield, I was separated from everyone else and led towards the rear of the plane. I was pulled up on to a luggage loader, an open platform skirted on three sides with rails and that was elevated to allow smoother transfer of luggage onto the plane. I was then elevated to the level of the back door, and I wheeled onto the plane and transferred into the last seat. I was in the smoking section so I could enjoy a few cigarettes. The flight to Melbourne was fairly routine, and upon arriving the procedure for the disembarking procedure was the same as in Alice Springs, but in reverse.

In Melbourne I phoned the two youth hostels listed and found out that neither were accessible. However, the staff person at one of the hostels assured me that there were only a few steps required to enter the hostel. I made a reservation and caught a taxi and went there only to discover that a few steps meant two flights of stairs. The hostel was located on the second floor. The taxi driver was nice enough to wait. Realizing the situation, he drove me to the other youth hostel, where there were only six steps, but I had to pass through three doors. I decided it was the better choice of the two, and I stayed.

I spent the remainder of the day and most of the next day sleeping. It felt like I was catching up on all the sleep that I had missed during my month-long stay.

The final evening I spent in Australia was memorable. Anna wanted to take me out for a special farewell dinner. Some friends had asked her to go to a concert that evening, but she chose to take me to dinner instead. Anna offered several choices, and asked me to choose one. I decided on Indian cuisine. Because cultures from all over the world are represented in Australia, there is a wide variety of ethnic cuisines. So when Anna presented the choices, I realized I had yet to enjoy Indian cuisine. Anna called the restaurant to make reservations, but because she normally didn't have to think about it, she neglected to find out the particulars about the accessibility of the restaurant. We arrived at the restaurant and discovered it was on the second floor. There was no elevator. Anna walked upstairs while I waited below. She was gone for quite some time.

After about fifteen minutes she returned, followed by two men and a woman. They apologized in broken English about the inconvenience, and agreed to pull me up the flight of stairs to the restaurant.

Because neither Anna nor I were familiar with the cuisine of India, we ordered what sounded somewhat tasty after the waiter had explained what the various dishes on the menu were. Anna ordered Bise Bele Hulianna and Lachchedar Paretage and I ordered Bise Bele Hulianna and Chicken Fry. We both had tea to drink and we split several Indian beer's, called LIONKING. It was a strong beer, and both of us felt the effects almost immediately. I was thinking back on my many adventures and I was feeling kind of reluctant about leaving Australia the next day. I had been considering the possibility of staying in Australia permanently, but did not have the whole plan thought out yet. I didn't know even if immigrating was an option, because I was an American citizen.

We had been looking at the many paintings in the restaurant and again I thought of the idea of staying in Australia, where I felt so free and comfortable. I turned to Anna and asked if there would be a way for us to maybe rent an apartment together. I was not thinking of anything permanent, or a physical relationship , although I would not have objected if the option arose. I thought it could be the ultimate ending and fulfillment of a lifelong dream of actually living in Australia. It would be the completion to the adventure.

I quickly made a mental calculation of the money I had left and I thought maybe I could pull this off for a few months, at least, and if I got some kind of employment in the counseling industry, I could stay there longer. I was thinking that it would be fun, and also financially more feasible for both of us to get a place together.

I was exhausted and feeling a bit worn around the edges from constantly being so open to the moment. It was very new to me, and I was feeling exposed and vulnerable. What she said was something that I had never expected.

"Thom, you are my friend and although I cannot say I like everything you have done while visiting me, I can say I love you and respect you. You have enormous amounts of courage to come to Australia in a wheelchair and do all the things that you have done. But, Thom, growing up here in Australia I have seen how all men treat women and I do not like it. I, myself, have been treated badly by men," she said.

"No, Thom, we cannot rent a place together. I do not like men."

I had not had a lot of exposure to people who were attracted to their own gender. I did not know if she meant that she was lesbian or she didn't want to get into a physical relationship with anyone. It was evident I had misrepresented myself. I truly saw that staying in Australia with Anna would be fun, risky and adventurous, and I was more than ready to move into a new area and purpose of my life.

What I heard was "Thom, I do not like you and the thought of getting a place with you I find disgusting." I was devastated. I couldn't think. My mind just shut down. These many years later I know this was not what she was really telling me. She really didn't say she didn't like me. She was talking more about herself than about me. But that is not the way I heard it at the time. I truly wish that I had been wiser and a little more in tune at the time we who spoke. I had grossly misunderstood what she meant. I wish I had not been so sensitive, that I had not been so tired and worn out and that I had handled the conversation differently. Looking back, I know now that I would have explained what I meant. Chances are, if I had, I would be living in Australia now.

That night I had a conversation with one of my bunkmates, who was backpacking through Australia in much the same fashion as myself. He was quite astonished that I was on my own and traveling through Australia. When I told him that I had begun my journey to Australia with just a round-trip ticket to Australia, he was blown away and said that even he had not come to Australia in such a bold fashion.

He had spent six months or so planning his trip and would not have the guts to make the trip that I had done.

I knew I needed to get up early to call the taxi that would take me to the airport. I set my little portable alarm clock and put it on the seat of my wheelchair and went to sleep fitfully, despite still being so tired. The next morning, when the alarm clock went off, I didn't want to wake up. I was in the middle of a dream that Anna had decided to take me up on my offer and we had gotten an apartment. I just laid there as the annoying ringing of the little alarm clock went off for a full minute, until it wound down, waking the other hostelers, who were bunking in the same room. I also had no desire to get up to make my way to the airport, especially with the disappointment of Anna's rejection. I did not want to leave the land of my dreams..

All through the remainder of my packing, through a hasty and bitter cup of stale coffee, that had been left on the heating coil for too long, through breakfast and the phone call to arrange my taxi to the airport, and all the way to the airport, the last conversation between Anna and I kept playing over and over in my head.

"I had not meant it the way she took it. But then, how had she taken it, I didn't even ask? All I meant was that it would be fun to get an apartment together, nothing physical, no intimate relationship, just two friends renting an apartment. Why had I not said something to correct her impression?"

The hustle and bustle of the airport and boarding the plane distracted me from my ruminations about whether or not I could have handled the conversation with Anna better.

This time I was able to sit in the bulkhead seat with plenty of leg room. The man behind the ticket counter did not give me any gruff about my seating choice and didn't think twice about giving me that seat. Maybe it was not in an emergency exit aisle.

On the flight home the plane was not full and I had the front row of seats to myself. Across the aisle from me was a nice middle-aged couple also returning from Australia to their home in Boston. We swapped stories and had many laughs. They had spent two weeks in Sydney and were quite taken with the Sydney Opera House. This is no lie. They were both musicians who played for the Boston Symphony. They were surprised when I told them about my travels to the many cities in Australia, how I got around, and how I began the trip. They were also quite amazed at my profession as a psychotherapist.

At one point in the flight I begin thinking about what had happened to me in Kings Cross, and started chuckling to myself. Under my breath, I kept repeating the words that Anna had spoken to me when I had woken up in the hospital.

"WHAT THE HELL AM I DOING IN AUSTRALIA?!"

"Excuse me," a flight attendant, who happened to be passing by said, mistakenly taking my words as something that I had said to her, stopped, leaned over, and asked "is everything all right."

"Yes, yes," I said, still chuckling to myself, "I was just thinking about something that happened to me when I was in Sydney." I briefly told her about my experience while in Kings Cross.

"You were in Sydney, also?" she asked, looking at me questioningly." Listen, I'm due for a break in about ten minutes. Would you mind if I joined you for a few minutes and you could tell me a little more about what you did in Australia? I noticed when you were boarding that you were in a wheelchair. I am studying architecture and would be interested in hearing some of your experiences and impressions of the accessibility issues you encountered during your stay"

"No, no, not at all. I would enjoy the company, especially from such a beautiful woman as yourself," I answered. "Thank you," she said, smiling at the complement.

I had a few moments to think as I waited for her to return. I remembered the time, many years ago, when I first became conscious of accessibility issues. Initially, access to buildings, or lack thereof, was not a big concern for me. My attitude was that there are always challenges in access, it's a fact of life, so why sweat it?

A few minutes later, she sat down next to me and asked for my thoughts on accessibility in Sydney and Melbourne.

I explained that my first impressions about accessibility happened when I was walking the streets in Alice Springs. "Most of the curbs are cut in Alice Springs," I said. "I was astonished, even in America you don't find this. Although, the curb cuts were quite steep, the fact of the matter is that they were cut."

"You were in Alice Springs? Where else were you in Australia?" she asked, trying to hide her disbelief.

I briefly told her the itinerary of the places I had been in Australia: Melbourne, Philip Island, Sydney, Adelaide, Alice Springs, and Uluru. Simply amazed, her jaw dropped and she just shook her head, then smiled.

"Obviously, there is more to this story than just accessibility," she said. "Tell me more about your travels."

So I did, starting with how it was I came to Australia with just a round-trip ticket, with no reservations, no tours planned, no rail tickets, no real plans other than simply coming to Australia. I told her how I felt when the plane landed and my first impressions of the people around me, whether they were Australian or other nationalities, of how open and friendly everyone seemed to be. I told her about my first encounter with the driving styles in Australia, rolling up to the wrong side of Anna's car and her chiding remark about whether I was going to drive.

"You guys, drive on the wrong side of the road," I said, laughing.

"Yes, I suppose we do, when you compare it with the backwards style of driving in America," she said, smiling and laughing. I got her punch and laughed.

She suddenly glanced at her watch and noting the time, she explained that her break was over and that she would come and sit with me again to hear more of the story. As it turned out though, she never did return to hear the rest of the story.

Actually, it was not important, she was the one who lost out. Because, in the end, I WENT TO AUSTRALIA.

Reference Web Sites

History of Vegemite

http://whatscookingamerica.net/History/VegemiteHistory.htm

Aboriginal Culture

http://www.pacificislandtravel.com/australia/about_destin/culture_aboriginals.asp

Oz Slang

http://www.pacificislandtravel.com/australia/about_destin/culture_dictionary.asp

Sydney Opera House

http://www.sydneyoperahouse.com/

Road-Trains

http://encyclopedia.thefreedictionary.com/Road%20train

Manly Beach

http://www.pacificislandtravel.com/australia/newsouthwales/syd_manlybeach.asp

Oceanworld

http://www.oceanworld.com.au/

Bondi Beach

http://www.voyeurmagic.com.au/

Foster' s Lager

http://www.australianbeers.com/beers/fosters/fosters.htm

Hangovers

http://www.australianbeers.com/beers/hangovers/hangovers.htm

Piss Beer

http://www.australianbeers.com/beers/piss/piss.htm

Didgeridoos

http://www.ididj.com.au/

Eucalyptus Trees

http://www.botanical.com/botanical/mgmh/e/eucaly14.html#med

Tree Kangaroo

http://home.iprimus.com.au/readman/lumh.htm

Koalas

http://www.savethekoala.com/koalasindex.html

Trains of Australia

http://www.australia.worldweb.com/Transportation/Trains/

Aboriginal art

http://www.aboriginalartshop.com/index.html

William Ricketts Sanctuary

http://teachit.acreekps.vic.edu.au/cyberfair2002/Williamrickettssanctuary.htm

City of Melbourne, Australia

http://www.melbourne.vic.gov.au/info.cfm?top=23&pg=966

Printed in the United States
130691LV00002B/38/A